ELLE HARTFORD

The Carousel Capers

To my wonderfully supportive partner, EMH,

who not only brought me to the quirky antiques store
where I found the first pair of carousel horse statuettes,

but also snuck back to said store to buy the remaining eight horses
as a surprise
after I'd struggled so valiantly to take home only two.

Contents

Bonus Prequel: Haunted Beauty

I like most people well enough, but I don't love very many people in this world. There's my family, of course, out there in the Sifting Sands. There's William, I suppose, the lost familiar turned travel partner—and business partner. But I've always been a rover, and aside from William's shaggy, dog-like self, not many have come along for the ride.

Still, if anything's for certain, it's that there's always exceptions. And I can tell you right now that I *adore* Dusty. I think I did almost from the moment he appeared in my newly-opened potions shop and began telling me all the gossip about Belville as though I'd lived there for years.

Dusty does all the maintenance for the shops around Market Square. That's how he excuses his tendency to pop up whenever you thought you just locked the front door, like he's some kind of poltergeist walking through walls. In fact, Dusty is a gnome—one as adept at hunting down free food as he is abysmal at picking out matching socks. Perpetually clad in baggy work overalls and a slouchy cap, with sparkling blue eyes and tan weathered skin, Dusty is a force to be reckoned with despite being about two and a half feet tall.

"You know, this ain't half bad, Red," Dusty told me one morning in late spring. He perched on my counter, his hands full of the herbed bread I'd just cooled and sliced. "That dog of yours's missing out."

"Not a dog," William mumbled from where he lay in the bay window, refusing to open his eyes before the crack of noon. It was a Rest day, and the shop was closed, so I didn't mind.

"Try it with the butter," I told Dusty, wiping my hands on my apron and offering him the little crock. When he looked suspicious, I added, "I didn't put garlic or salt in it this time. Goodness take me for trying to bring a little culinary sophistication to the wilds of Pastoria!"

Dusty raised his eyebrows at his last remaining piece of bread. Half my loaf had gone. "I think the wilds'd rather be left as they are. Did I tell you 'bout the work site last night?"

"No, what happened?" I leaned on the kitchen island that doubled as a dining table in my tiny apartment and waited, grinning to myself as I wondered, *when does he think he might have told me anything? He only showed up just in time to start wolfing down bread!*

"Not sure," Dusty said, in that tone of voice which I'd learned indicated he had a good deal to say on the subject. He hesitated before continuing, "I told you that after that big storm a few days ago, th' Council hired me'n some others to fix th' bridge out on South Road?"

I nodded. The storm in question had been not big but huge: lightning, thunder, downed trees—the whole bit. Dusty had been very busy since then.

"I was a bit late leaving, because some people can't be trusted t' clean up after themselves." Whenever he disapproved, Dusty made his comments very mildly. "It was dark, an' somethin' screeched, an' I turned round to find a person's skull sitting right behind me."

My mouth dropped open. "You found a *what*?"

From his place at the window, William sneezed. With one eye cracked open, he said, "Is the gnome's discovery the reason Thorn is tromping around to the shop's back entrance as you speak?"

"What?" I repeated before setting my hands on my hips and narrowing my eyes at Dusty. "You set me up."

Dusty shrugged as he buttered another piece of bread. "I jus' told her she could probably find me here. You don't mind, do you, Red? My place's a mess, you know."

I *didn't* know, because I had no idea where Dusty's place was. It occurred to me that perhaps, like an opportunistic cat, Dusty simply floated from house to house. But I had no time to dwell on this because a loud knock sounded and a louder voice followed:

"Officer Thorn reporting! I know you're in there, Red, I can smell whatever you've got baking from out here. If you don't let me in, I'll—oh, good morning. No need to look so serious! Get it? Knead? Ha, ha." Officer Thorn grinned toothily as she invited herself in, and followed me up the narrow back steps to the apartment. I knew exactly where this was headed, so I busied myself cutting up the rest of the bread as the police officer spied Dusty and said, "Aha, there's our resident ghostbuster, eh?"

"Ghosts don't have skulls." William still hadn't risen: between him and the broad-shouldered, green-skinned half-orc Officer, bickering was a familiar pastime.

"Already heard the story, have you? Good, I want to get an early start so Red and I have plenty of time to look around." When silence reigned—stunned on my part, ambivalent on the part of my good-for-nothing companions—Officer Thorn added, "I'll take no guff on this, now. Dusty's find could be evidence of murder or, even worse, occult activity. We take these things seriously in Belville. The last time something like this happened, all our farms were taken over by a viney ooze and we lost three horses, a family of pigs, and the old mayor."

I chose not to wonder what it said about the past mayor that their life was apparently on par with a bunch of swine. Instead I turned, offering Thorn a piece of bread on an old wooden plate. "And why do I need to go along *this* time?"

Officer Thorn accepted the bread graciously, sweeping back gorgeous black hair before taking a huge bite. "Just as good as it smells," she declared happily. Then, more pertinently, "Because, Miss Alchemist, it wasn't just any skull. It was a *preserved* skull. Sure to be full of chemicals and all kinds of things right up your alley. Besides, who knows what else is there? Did Dusty tell you about the castle yet?"

* * *

Since the day Officer Thorn had decided that the new alchemist in town (me) would make the perfect unofficial crime-fighting sidekick, I'd solved a grand total of three cases and dealt with exactly zero bodies. I was familiar with death, of course, as much as anyone else who's lived; but all the same,

I'll admit I was a little leery of going back to the place where Dusty had made his gruesome discovery.

Even if it *was* to make sure Dusty hadn't stumbled upon some curse that might put him in danger.

Officer Thorn and I followed South Road through the forest, which went from light and airy to dense and feral to dark and foreboding as though we weren't walking so much as sliding along a scale. At a crook in the road following the contour of a ravine, we found the broken bridge. And up the hillside from that bridge was another casualty of the storm: a massive, ancient tree, which had fallen directly down the slope. Its trunk had crashed through a section of wooden wall that would have been otherwise invisible, hidden in brambles. But in the space left by the giant tree's demise, we could see not only the wall but a glimpse of the castle it had been hiding.

Officer Thorn whistled, long and low. "*That's* been there a while, eh?"

Against my better judgment, I scrambled up onto the downed tree to get a better look. The castle was set back from the wall, at the top of the hill: if I titled my head right, I could see one wooden turret outlined against the sky. It looked *exactly* like a haunted ruin, and I knew what to do with those. I turned back down the hill at once, ready to leave—

And, naturally, my foot dislodged the skull which Dusty had left in place the night before.

Officer Thorn caught it deftly, like I had tossed her a ball. "What d'ya think? Any guess what's been done to it?" And she lobbed it back in my direction.

"Urgh," I said as I caught the thing, clumsily. "For the record, I deal with *natural* sciences, like geology and botany. I am not a mad scientist used to performing creepy experiments."

"Uh-huh," said Officer Thorn, her hands tucked into her dapper uniform with a cheerful air. "So would any sciences you know of make a skull look like *that?*"

I squinted at the skull, turning it over in my hands and lifting it into the streaked daylight, finally pulling my ever-present goggles from my forehead down over my eyes in order to check for residues and fractures. At last I slid from the tree trunk and pressed the gruesome thing back into the Officer's hands, saying, "Well, I don't think it's anyone you know—unless you're much older than you look. As far as I can tell, this thing is human, male, riddled with toothache, and undeniably ancient. And that isn't chemicals on it—it's traces of *Ptilium crista-castrensis.*"

Thorn gave me an expectant look, and I sighed. "It's moss, Officer."

"I knew I was right to pick you as my new unofficial partner," Thorn announced, tucking the skull into her knapsack and clapping me on the shoulder. "Keep an eye out for things more'n moss as we investigate!"

"'Investigate'? In *there?*" I hesitated, but Officer Thorn was already walking up the tree trunk like a tightrope, alighting in the unkempt castle yard beyond the fence. I could leave her alone to her folly, or I could explore the ruin. *At least it's broad daylight,* I thought. It's not that I'm particularly superstitious, but everyone in Beyond knows better than to tempt fate.

Well, most of us do, anyway. Officer Thorn strode right up to the castle and shouldered her way through the once-grand, now-rotted front door without so much as a "watch out ghosts, here I come!".

I followed her into the gloom. Outside had been a nice spring day, but the atmosphere in the castle was icy. The main hallway was huge, with a vaulted ceiling and sconces along the walls. Doorways carved in what looked like arched tree designs branched off in all directions. Everything was made of various types of wood, inlaid with tiles and gems. Though I had had my reservations about the cobwebby, soundless space, I found it difficult not to stray from Officer Thorn's company in order to examine the walls around us.

Ahead, Thorn grunted. "Not very dusty."

"Hm?" It took me a moment to realize she meant actual dirt, not the gnome who'd sent us there. "Well it's a little hard to tell in the dark. Don't you have a light?"

"That's an alchemy thing," the Officer replied breezily. As though daring me to contradict her, she added, "Don't you sell lightsticks in your shop?"

"I do," I said, trying both not to whisper—as she seemed determined not to do—and not to grind my teeth. "You should consider buying some."

"Always a businesswoman!" Officer Thorn chuckled as she continued walking. "Come on, there's skylights up ahead."

Annoying as she was, she was also right. The hallway opened up into a rounded interior courtyard of sorts, with grimy, broken skylights set into a rounded ceiling. A railed hallway, or maybe two, marked out the different stories above us. Even with my exceptional dark vision, it was difficult to discern any detail in the smeared, greenish light. The darkness at my back pressed upon me. I *hate* confined spaces where I don't know of at least two exits.

Calm down, it's fine, I reminded myself, trying to take deep breaths and be still the way my mother had taught me as a child. *Listen,* she would say. *Won't you ever listen, little cinnabar?*

My eyes snapped open. I'd listened, and I'd heard an eerie

music floating in the stagnant air.

"Thorn," I hissed. "What day is it?"

"Acorn Festival, maybe?" Thorn still spoke at her normal, sure-to-disturb-any-nearby-miscreants volume. She'd wandered into the center of the room, poking at large plant-filled urns with her boot. "I dunno, I can never keep all the town holidays and festivals strai—"

"No, no—I meant, what phase of the moon is it. Is it New Moon yet?"

Officer Thorn looked back at me thoughtfully, her hand on her hip. "Think we have a few days yet before that."

"Hmm." The music I heard—or thought I heard—reminded me of the echoey tones most moon-worshiping cults like. But before I could ask Officer Thorn if she heard it too, it vanished.

* * *

"And that was about it," I told William later over a thick spiced stew. It's not that I was unnerved about the castle—sometimes, a person just needs comfort food. "We poked around a little more, and in an alcove I found some parchment with old records. It's in a weird dialect though, so Thorn said she was going to take it—and the skull—to the lady who runs the curio shop. Priya, I think?"

William lifted his nose out of his bowl to snort. "What's *she* supposed to do?"

"Officer Thorn thought she might have seen similar things before. Apparently she runs a museum in her basement. We should go see it sometime; it's only right across the square. What?"

"I just don't see how anyone that obsessed with being part-fairy could have much to say about arcane castles."

"If you wanted us to ask you instead, you should have come along," I told him. I had only met Priya once, and remembered her as a pleasant, if slightly commanding, person. Come to think of it though she *had* mentioned fairies. Or had it been druids?

I shook my head, dismissing the matter as unimportant. William knew a great deal about our neighbors, for spending so much of his time asleep.

"So that's it?" he asked, still curious despite his natural grumpiness. "It's just somebody's forgotten house?"

"Hardly just a house. Thorn still seems to think it might unleash some sort of curse on the town. It wouldn't surprise me, honestly." I paused. I hadn't told William that at one point, I thought for sure I'd seen light green eyes watching me—because really, I thought, it was probably just more gems set into the wall. People who build castles have weird senses of humor.

"I don't see why that should stop them rebuilding the bridge and going about with their business."

I flicked his ear. "Try to be nice, won't you? A curse could be a big deal. For—"

A knock at the door below interrupted me. I rose and went downstairs, through the shop, to find Officer Thorn standing at my front stoop.

"No time to go around the back," she explained. "Saw your lights on. I hope you're done with your dinner, because Dusty's family has reported him missing, and I think we both know where he might have gotten to."

As I stood gaping, William stuck his head around my leg.

"Don't worry. Red can smell missing people from miles away; when we met she was a private investigator for a Queen. And this time, I'm coming along to see that castle for myself!"

* * *

William may have a penchant for stretching (or straight-up inventing) the truth, but he also has good instincts. He'd been loping along in front of Officer Thorn, who was in turn closely followed by me; but the moment we neared the ancient castle's doors, he skidded to a halt that had us all tumbling like dominoes.

"*Mihi nihil nocer—*"

"What's that, then?" Officer Thorn picked herself up first and interrupted William's muttering. He barked back at her,

"Introductions! Don't you have any manners?"

I dusted off my tunic and trousers and struggled not to reprimand them for arguing while who knew *what* might be happening to Dusty inside. Most moon-cults were peaceful, but some did still believe that nothing greased the cosmic gears better than blood. And the more I thought about the music I'd heard earlier, the tighter the knot in the pit of my stomach became.

William glowed a starry blue as he finished whatever magic he was working on the castle door. Behind him, I couldn't help but tap my feet—and he heard it.

"Go on, then," William told me, jerking his wet black nose toward the door. "First one in gets the honor of setting off all the trapdoors. Be it upon your head."

"I know, I know." Really, what else could one expect from

an abandoned castle at night but tricks and traps? As I passed William I added more gently, "We're going to be fine."

"There's that can-do attitude," Officer Thorn piped up, following me into the castle. I shivered as I passed inside, but she seemed unaffected as she suggested, "We got three people, which means three teams. One of us can—"

"No!" William and I interrupted at once. "No splitting up!"

Officer Thorn paused as though she might argue. She watched the heavy castle door close behind us, the last rays of starlight fading and ending with a snap. "Very well then, onward it is," she decided.

All three of us could see in the dark, but all the same I passed out lightsticks and Revealing Powder. At least the lights would help Dusty; I wasn't sure if gnomes had good dark vision. Officer Thorn led the way into one room after another, more quietly than I would have imagined possible. I followed, keeping a careful eye out for shadows, and an ear out for sounds.

"Red," William whispered from behind me. "Red, I don't like these tapestries. They're hiding something. They could be watching us."

"The pictures?" I hadn't looked closely at them, but I glanced at one as Officer Thorn paused in a doorway. It didn't look like anything other than pastoral art. But out of the corner of my eye, I saw the one next to it shimmer.

"This would be a good time to do the Seer thing for once, Red," William said, pressing against the back of my legs.

"Hush!" I looked over at Thorn, but she hadn't heard; she was motioning us into the next room, a smaller exterior hallway of sorts. As we crept after her, I reminded William, "That's not how 'the Seer thing' works."

William's fluffy tail shook with the end of a shiver. "It'd work better than waiting for whatever's moving in here to catch up with us."

I scanned the hallway in lonely shades of blue to no avail: I didn't have the arcane sense that William did. "Can't you tell what it is?"

"Cursed thing's too slippery," he muttered back. "Go catch up with Thorn: she went into the next room already."

"Too *slippery*? That doesn't sound like—"

My mind flickered, slow to reconcile thoughts. My memories of the last time William and I had encountered a moon cult, and his description of their magics as "filtery," not "slippery," mixed with my confusion about what else might be in the castle and why, which collided headlong with my realization that Officer Thorn was nowhere to be seen.

I'd traced her steps into the next room, just as William had suggested. The room appeared to be a kind of library, but the shelves were filled with large, rough scrolls and the tables stood at chest height. There was nothing, no doors ajar, no overturned chairs, no cabinets to hide behind—nothing except a very large fireplace to one side.

"William, I can't see Thorn!"

The ex-familiar squeezed through the doorway around me and looked around, panting as he tasted the air. When he spotted the fireplace, he groaned. "What do you want to bet it's a rotating fireplace? She *would* be one to fall for that."

"Yes, well, we need to figure out how," I said, cracking a lightstick to create a yellow glow in the emptiness. As I moved to the fireplace, now having lost *two* friends, I realized that William was probably right. I needed to be doing everything I possibly could. Even if that meant tapping into powers and traditions I'd wanted to leave behind.

I set the lightstick on the mantle and stepped back, shoving my goggles farther up my forehead. The light was distracting: I retreated farther into the shadow. I went still, breathed deep. I could hear William as he investigated the hearth. I could feel the air drifting past my shoulder blades. I could see—

But I paused, distracted. Air was moving? Where to? I looked to my right and there, hidden in the corner, I saw a doorway cracked open. It was on the same wall as the fireplace: if Thorn hadn't used the door herself, then it might open into whatever room she had entered by dramatic means of fireplace. Not stopping to wonder why there'd be a trapdoor and a real door going to the same place, I called to William and drifted forward, into the corner and over the threshold.

For a moment all I could see was waves. Waves of shadow, shifting and crashing and shaping each other. I shook my head, blinking back the meditative practice my mother had taught me, trying to focus on what was *there*.

What was there, I soon found, was not nothing. I was in a chamber along the outer wall of the castle: old, dirty windows provided uncertain moonlight. The rays crossed over woven rugs and a broken desk before landing on a form that would have been human if it wasn't a head too tall.

"Goddess protect me," I whispered softly to myself. I couldn't make out any details about the stranger in the room—other than eyes so light green they seemed to glow in the dark.

Right when I realized that the door behind me had closed and a crash resounded from the room I'd left William in, the form rippled and spoke in a low voice. "I mean you no harm, Rrred."

"William!" Something inside me flashed, and my frayed

nerves gave way. "That is *it*," I exclaimed. "Does *every* stranger in town know my name? Doesn't anyone in Belville start conversations by saying something about *themselves*? If I didn't know any better, I'd think you all were in some sort of league of secrets!"

The voice hesitated—and then chuckled. "Forgive me for thinking you might be afraid, and wishing to allay your fearrs."

"Then why'd you lock me in here? Where is Dusty, and William and Officer Thorn? Whatever you're doing with them, stop it this instant. And tell me who you are and what you want!"

"I have not done anything with them." The form shrugged, as though such an inane gesture could prove its innocence. "But I may know where they arre, and I can take you to them in just a moment."

I crossed my arms. "But?"

"'But'?"

"But *what*," I prompted. "There was a catch in there, and if you think you're keeping *that* secret too, you've got another think coming."

The creature, whatever it was, spoke earnestly. "I wish to speak to you. I have followed not them, but *you*. I am a frriend, I prromise."

"Oh, *curse* it." Suddenly I realized why all those rolled *rs* sounded familiar: I'd spoken to this corporeally-challenged mystery "friend" when investigating the hut of a dead Witch several moons before. If I hadn't been itching so badly to dive out the nearest window, I would have caught on sooner. "Well, right now, my priority is helping the friends that are lost somewhere in this awful castle, so I'm going to go look for them. We can talk about your terrible timing and whatever else you want to say later."

"Wait, Rrred," said the shadow, and I did, because it sounded more serious than before. "You must be careful; this castle is cursed, more so even than your friend Thorn suspects. There is evil at work here. It will eat away your sense of time, and drain your sense of self. When you leave, you must not return.

"But in the meantime I will take you to your frrriends," it ended, more softly, "because I am herre to help you."

The lanky enigma shuddered toward a door I hadn't noticed before, and then glided through the next hallway to an exterior door.

I hesitated before leaving the castle. "Are you sure going *out* is the answer?"

The green eyes blinked. Even in the moonlight, faint as it was, I could see no more. "We will go around the outside of the castle, and through a lower entrance."

I nodded, stepping out. In the night air I breathed more freely, and we raced around the side of the sprawling building. "Do you live here?" I asked, suddenly curious.

"I?" The shadow wavered. "No, I do not live here. I came herre, as you did. And that is what I want you to know, Rrred: that you are not alone."

Before I could think, much less argue, my escort gestured to an open cellar door and a damp—but suspiciously clean—set of stairs. I heard William *woof* in the darkness beyond them, and without hesitation I dove into the castle basement, shouting as I went,

"Whatever it is that's going on, stop it this instant!"

I was met with silence (aside from a very small noise that I suspected might be a chuckle from behind me). For a moment I, too, was silent, because the basement beneath the castle wasn't a *basement* at all.

The floor beneath us was level, earthen, and seemed to extend as far and wide as the castle itself. It was difficult to say for certain, though, because everywhere around us pillars sprouted up from the ground and reached into the ceiling. They were illuminated by faint, dancing green lights of every shade. I could see why my mystery friend had called this space "the lower courtyard." It smelled dewy and alive.

And that green light illuminated not only the pillars, but a clearing of sorts in which stood William, Dusty, Officer Thorn, and a ring of hooded—and I must say, very perturbed—figures.

Without wondering what a moon cult might be doing underground—because as nice as this space was, it definitely didn't have a view of the sky—I strode forward. The hooded figures circled around a rough stone altar of sorts, on which Dusty was sitting; William had leapt up beside him, but Thorn was standing behind, as though she'd come from that direction. Indeed, when I looked into the shadowy pillars beyond her, I could see what looked like a crumpled ladder.

But now wasn't the time for worrying about that. I accosted the nearest brown-robed figure, catching hold of their hood before they could scurry away. "What in Beyond is going on here?"

"Unhand that acolyte!" demanded the figure nearest the altar. "Remember, there are more of us than of you. And *you* are the one who has trespassed!"

"Is that so," Officer Thorn piped up. "I'd like to see a deed of ownership for this castle, in that case."

"You trespassed on our *ritual*," said the robed figure, sounding more than a little exasperated.

"You stole our friend!" I retorted.

"And as of now, you stand accused of plotting against the Council!" added Officer Thorn.

"— you have interrupted holy rites —"

"You had something follow us!" barked William.

I cocked my head as the confrontation devolved into schoolyard accusations. While alleged crimes were hurled like dodge balls, I wondered if I could sneak under the din and get Dusty out of there. He sat unnaturally still: he'd definitely been bound, though I couldn't tell with what.

"We haven't done anything, and you have no evidence against us!" hollered the ritual leader.

"I have a trussed-up gnome that says different!" Officer Thorn boomed back.

I decided to go for it. None of the other robed figures were paying me any mind; they seemed transfixed by the shouting match. I made it to the altar without anyone coming at me or making any comment.

"We wouldn't have hurt him!"

"Then why'd you bother to abduct him?" William wondered.

"We just—wanted to scare him a little," the robed leader mumbled.

I reached Dusty and began removing his bonds, which turned out to be rough, hempen rope. He wasn't unscathed, but he beamed at me with some of his usual spirit.

"Right, that's enough," Officer Thorn decided. "I hereby declare your little party over."

"You ruined it anyway," the leader continued to mumble under her breath.

"I'm going to need the name of your order and its purpose. And while we're at it, I want everyone's name and place of—"

Officer Thorn's words were drowned out as a veritable

stampede began. Acolytes went running in every direction, not unlike children playing a round of "kick the can." I huddled closer to the altar, William, and Dusty. Officer Thorn lunged for the leader and came up with a handful of candle wax and a necklace of wooden beads, which spilled limply from her hand.

"Don't worry," William told the officer, once he'd finished laughing and every last one of the cultists had disappeared. "We already know everything about them that we need to."

"'Sat so?" Dusty rubbed at his wrists, still looking to the basement door—the one I'd arrived by, and the kidnappers had disappeared out of. "I never saw nothin' myself. All that cult business is mumbo-jumbo to me."

Officer Thorn made a sound of exasperation at the averred uselessness of her one eyewitness while William shook his head in amusement. "It's the Festival of the Acorn and the Oak," he reminded us. "Brown robes? Green candles? Sheesh, do you all need *everything* spelled out for you?"

"If you're going to be high and mighty, then *you* can be Officer Thorn's assistant," I told him smartly. "Dusty and I are getting out of here."

"It's a good thing you knew about that outer door, Red," Dusty said as we began walking. "Did you know your dog there broke the ladder from the fireplace?"

I resisted the urge to hit my forehead with the palm of my hand. "There was a ladder in the fireplace?" *How did I miss that?*

"That's about when I came to, when we was goin' down," said Dusty easily. "Then everything got interrupted when William fell through."

I set aside all thoughts about the ritual for a moment, and

focused on my friend. "I'm sorry you had to go through that, Dusty. Were you scared?"

"Scared?" Dusty looked up at me, grinning crookedly. "Never. Just think of the stories I'll be able to tell now!"

* * *

It turned out William had indeed recognized the cult—a fact he wasn't likely to let me or Officer Thorn forget for some time. He declined to become yet another police assistant (and how he had success doing so is beyond me, but I wish he would have shared the secret) but he did tell us all about the druidic Order of the Holy Oak. Based on William's deductions and a glass slipper-like search for the other half of the broken necklace, Officer Thorn soon had the cult's leader in custody.

"Priya! I told you she was suspicious," William reminded me, not for the first time, as we cleaned up the shop after yet another day of business.

"Maybe so," I agreed, wincing over the fact that I had never connected Priya's talk about druids with the ethereal music and forest themes I'd observed at the castle. "But Dusty doesn't seem too upset over the whole thing, and there's no law against strange basement rituals, as long as no one gets hurt."

William snorted. "She deserves a full trial, after what she had following us."

"Nice to see you so worried about your friend Dusty," I replied, teasing him. "You know, the gnome who got actually abducted, and is the real victim here?"

But William ignored my point. "I'm not kidding around, Red! That thing was *creepy!*"

"Are you sure?" I set down my broom. In the glowing evening light, the shadows of my shop were gilded, and my memories of the castle felt less perilous. I gazed off in thought, saying slowly, "I think I may have met it."

"You *met* it?!"

"When you fell down the fireplace. Nice going on that, by the way. You told me to do the Seer thing, so I tried, but then I realized there was another room. I tried to tell you, but in the end it was just me and . . . it."

"Oh, gods." William heaved his upper body onto the sales counter, flopping one large paw over his face for full effect. "Don't tell me. You're friends with it now."

"It helped me find you," I pointed out, clutching my broom handle.

"*Red!* If you found an angry red djinn on the road and it promised you water, would you befriend *that,* too?"

"You shouldn't be so judgmental. I befriended *you,* and I think that's worked out pretty well for you so far," I reminded William. He snorted.

"*I* am a powerful and interesting benevolent being with a great sense of humor. And the creep in the castle is . . . ?"

"I don't know yet," I answered truthfully. "It's tall. It moves pretty fast. And it has bright green eyes. And it said it doesn't live in the castle. It . . ."

"Great," William said, not needing me to finish my ill-conceived sentence to realize where I'd been headed. "It follows us around. And it's tall, you say? Gods know all great friendships have been based on height!"

"Stop being annoying," I told him as he stood up on his front paws on the counter. "It's easy to be so dismissive of a thing when you don't have a name for it. I think, for now, we should call it . . . Jade."

"Sure, it *said* it doesn't live in the castle," William grumbled, though he followed me upstairs. "Anyone can say anything. If you ask me, a better name for the thing would be *Beast*."

I paused on the landing to our apartment. "You may be right," I admitted. It's true I felt like not everything with the castle had been resolved. But all the same, I straightened and added, "Only time will tell. For now, the castle can go back to being quiet and abandoned, Officer Thorn's keeping an eye on Priya and her acolytes, and Dusty can get back to building bridges and snitching food. I think we deserve to take a break from worrying. What are we having for supper?"

William heaved a sigh at me, but I paid him no mind. I knew he cared for Dusty as much as I did, and furthermore, I knew he thought I was right. We needed a break.

Of course, at that time, I had no idea that hauntings and curses never *truly* go away until you face them head on . . .

. . . And in my rush to save my friend, I'd forgotten entirely about the skull that started the whole affair.

1

A Blue Shade

The First Carousel Caper

In the world of Beyond, every country is "once upon a time" and "far, far away." Moving from one to the next is like leaping through a wormhole to another planet: from fairy tale castles to pirate-infested waters, then on to alien landscapes or magitech cities. With magic and a little bit of luck on your side, you can go anywhere, except of course for the afterlife (or at least, that particular trip doesn't come with a return ticket).

Anyway, I'm the perfect person to talk about travel, because I've been almost everywhere. Born the child of mystic Seers, I'm an alchemist by trade, and only recently stopped roaming Beyond to set up a potions shop in small-town Belville. Ironically, though, the focus of this story is the epitome of staying in one place. This is a story about a cursed carousel horse.

Not exactly a formidable beginning, right? And not only a carousel horse, but a tiny one at that. A child's toy. Normally I'm happy to find humor in anything—my mother would always say "it's hard not to look on the bright side when you live in the desert," something I remember with much more fondness now that I've started a new life far from home—but the truth is, this business with the carousel horse started on a more serious note.

A letter, in fact. Scrawled in the worst handwriting since the very first person picked up a quill, written on an old piece of parchment crumpled around a small blue horse, it read:

"Red old friend stopping by Belville have a nole to look at will follow afternoon. Oold times sake, counting on you"

It ended just like that, abruptly. And though the note and the horse showed up on my doorstep in the mail, my old friend—whoever they might be—never came.

* * *

"Red. Look at me. Red."

I shook my head, letting the world filter back into place. I sat on what might have been a stack of books in Owl's overstuffed bookshop, one hand buried in my cloak clutching that strange little horse. The shop sounded empty, quiet, and smelled like leather book covers. The clerk knelt in front of me with a tome clutched to his chest like a talisman, and from under his scholar's hood he regarded me with patience.

"Sorry." I sucked in a breath, reminding myself that I'd gone to the bookstore for information. Three days I'd been carrying that horse around in my pocket, wondering where

2

my sense of foreboding was coming from. I'd even begun to imagine people watching me from behind lampposts on Belville's cobbled streets. It was past time to learn about my new "toy." "I was spacing out. Thanks, um—sorry, I never asked your name?"

"It's fine, I only gave you the discount of the year on a potions book the last time you came in," said the clerk, his green eyes alight. "I mean really though, don't feel bad, most people in town just know me as 'Owl's assistant.'" He sat back on his heels and stuck out a dark-skinned hand. "I'm Luca."

"Red," I said, returning the gesture automatically. Copper—that's how I've always thought of my skin. With obsidian hair and a protective shell of lab gear and really, is it any wonder I became an alchemist? Luca shook my hand and that small gesture banished the last of my wayward thoughts. I smiled back at him. "Of course, you already knew that, just like everyone else in town."

"And miles around, most likely. That's the price of being a mysterious stranger who practices alchemy," he told me. "Are you sure you're okay?"

"I'm fine." But the horse and the baffling note had thrown me off my game, making me hesitate. I sighed at my obvious lie and added, "Or anyway, I will be. So, did you find anything on carousel horses? Or charms maybe?"

"Well, I couldn't find any definition or reference for 'nole.' And nothing on carousel horses either," Luca said, his voice full of apology. "I mean, unless you want a kid's story, which I don't think is what you were looking for? So, in that case, the closest I could come was this encyclopedia of water charms and focuses. You said the horse you're researching is blue, right?"

"Yeah," I said, shifting uncomfortably on my stool. "But why would a carousel have anything to do with water?"

"I don't know, but then, you never *do* know, right?" Luca handed me the book he'd been holding, and flopped onto the dusty floor as I perused it. "Even if it doesn't help exactly, it might give you some ideas for where to look next," he said. I bit my cheek, half-listening as he continued, "I could look up some old scrolls on statues—I'm pretty sure we have some in the art section—most of them are just a catalog of historic artifacts, but maybe if the object you have is historically significant, then—"

"It's just a trinket," I corrected automatically, before glancing from the pages to Luca. "Unless there's some famous series of old horse-themed artifacts out there that I've never heard of?"

"Well, no, not that I know of either, but I figure it never hurts to try." As Luca spoke, my fingers tightened around the horse. I had described it to Luca, but I hadn't shown it to anyone yet. *Maybe I'm being paranoid,* I thought. *Maybe I should take it over to the antiquities shop and see if they know what it is.* Meanwhile, Luca was still talking. "—now, you did mention charms, and if there's magic in it, maybe it *is* an artifact—not a historic one but a magical one. You know, like the kind Owl would call a 'storied ritualistic object'?"

"Um . . . no, I don't." Scholar-speak has never been my strong suit.

"No one really does," said Luca cheerfully. "Close as I can tell, it means that the object is attached to a myth of some kind, and that myth gives it power to weave a very particular charm. A charm most likely associated with the myth. Am I just rambling, you think?"

* * *

By the time Luca had run out of topics to ramble about, my lunch hour was over. I hastily thanked him and half-walked, half-ran back to my own shop on Belville's Market Square.

My store, "Red's Alchemy and Potions," really was a dream come true. It sat at one corner of the tree-dotted Square, with glittering bay windows and a tidy front step. On the first floor were potions, ingredients, and all kinds of inventions for sale; on the second floor was my tiny apartment, which I shared with a magic familiar named William. Despite his appearance as a big, hairy black dog, he was an arcane being full of his own ideas. And during my trip to the bookstore he'd been in charge of my shop on his own long enough to cause trouble, so I hurried home through the summer heat.

Fortunately, the shop was still standing and the rest of the afternoon went smoothly. But my attempt at "researching" the little horse had left me with more questions than before. That night over a fragrant dinner of curry and rice, I told William everything Luca had said. And, against my own better judgment, I finally let my magically-inclined companion see the strange gift I'd found in the mail.

William, who often sat on a chair at the tiny dining table with me despite the fact that he rarely ate my dinners and was far too huge and furry for my apartment-sized furniture, looked down at the horse and growled. "And you didn't show this to me in the beginning because . . . ?"

I stared at my plate. The horse, made of deep blue stone and gilded gold mane, tail, and accents—complete with carousel pole—pranced in my peripheral vision. It was only as tall as my palm. But the words of the note echoed in my mind, heavy with allusions to "old times." I had thought I'd left my past behind me when I settled in Belville. It's not that I had anything to be ashamed of, exactly, but I was trying to start a new chapter in my life, trying to focus on my business. *Not* on some wild carousel-horse chase.

"Because I wasn't sure what it was," I said finally, sighing. "And I didn't want to get you into trouble. I think—well, I had a bad feeling about it at first, and now that no one has shown up, I think whoever sent it is in danger."

William sneezed. "Or they *are* the danger." Scorn aside, though, he lowered his head to look properly at the horse. "What's it made of?"

The question surprised me. I had figured that, in his arcane vision, it'd become clear that the thing was made of ancient magic and racing nightmares, or something like that. I hadn't even examined it closely myself. But since he asked, I pushed aside my half-eaten meal and pulled my alchemists' goggles, always plastered on my forehead no matter where I am, over my eyes. "At first glance I'd say polished azurite. The stone isn't very hard—you can see scratching if you look closely. I think the gold is real."

"And the bookstore guy couldn't find any reference to it?"

"He suggested looking into historic artifacts. Or, oddly enough, water charms." Suddenly thinking of the scratches on the horse's neck, like a person clawing for air, I set it down and started cleaning up my dinner.

William watched me as I wiped down the kitchen island, stowed my leftovers in a small, enchanted icebox, and piled dishes in the sink. "Did you show it to him?"

"No. What do you think, I've been running around flashing

it to everyone?"

"There's a joke there." William's tail thumped, but just as quickly he turned solemn again. "At least you have *some* discretion. Even if you didn't catch on to the fact that it's suspicious how he knew to suggest water charms and storied objects."

"He was just throwing out ideas. So?" As I said the words, I looked out into the darkness. The kitchen occupied the upper corner of my building, so I had a window in front of me at the sink and one behind William in the dining nook. When moving in, I had liked how light the place could be, but now the windows made me shiver. "I thought you were friends with Owl, and now you suspect his assistant of—of what, exactly?"

"I'm just saying, it's weird how much they know sometimes," William said. "You never know, maybe there's a crime ring out there after this horse, and they've recruited Owl and his assistant."

My hands slipped on the soapy dishes. "You sound like Officer Thorn."

"Yeah, well, anyone who talks as much as she does has to be right *some* of the time." William shook himself and glowed momentarily, a starry blue light I knew well. It meant he was strengthening the protections he kept up around our home. "Red. If it's a myth, then I know which one it is."

This time I dropped the plate altogether. "You *what?*"

"Starting to think maybe you should have come to me at the start, eh?" he asked smugly. When I turned to him, putting wet hands on my hips, he let out a canine whine. "Oh come on, how could I *not* know about a mythical creature? I am one, you know."

"You're a familiar who somehow lost his sorcerer and now

spends most of his time sleeping," I retorted good-humoredly as I moved back to the table and spun a chair around, sitting astride it. "Spill. What do you know?"

"I never get any respect," William murmured. "First of all, look at it again. Those aren't hooves, they're too long and flat. They're little fins. And the tail is too long and thin for a horse."

"I figured it was artistic license."

"You weren't looking, because you didn't want to. It's a *caballo marino*. You don't recognize the name? What do they even teach you in alchemy school? How about a *bunyip*? A *wihwin*? A nixie, a backahast, a kelpie?"

"First of all, I didn't go to school for alchemy, I apprenticed. Second, you know *you're* the expert on occult matters around here, and third—you're just pulling my leg."

"I am not. That's what *these* things do." William gestured to the little horse with his nose, and sniffed at my other comments. "They trick people into touching them, and once you've touched it then you're locked on and it drags you down into the water. Sometimes it eats you, too. Other people say it's a way for sorcerers to get to ghost ships."

"Oooookay." I looked at the statuette again. It did have a marine look. "Are you saying that this *is* one? Or just that it's a whaddyacallit attached to the myth?"

"Of course it isn't one, not literally. Don't be ridiculous. But it is *something*," William said, abruptly pushing it over the table toward me. "It's got something inside it, some charm I can't see."

"So if we break it open, you'll know what it is?"

"Why are you so literal, Red? If you break this statue, you'll just let whatever the spell is *out* before we have time to prepare a defense."

"Okay, so, no breaking the weird carousel seahorse," I said as I stood and stretched. "If that's all the wisdom you have to share tonight, I'm going to bed. Tomorrow morning I'll go see Thorn and get her take on the horse, the note, everything. So if you want to come along, get your rest now while you can."

* * *

The next morning technically marked the beginning of the Rest Day, but I didn't spare much time for relaxation. Officer Thorn, Belville's one and only police officer, lived and worked at the station on the edge of town. It was only a ten minute walk from my shop to the squat, wooden building. In the early morning sunlight, Belville's police station looked like a deflated guard tower still striving to keep the forest at bay.

Officer Thorn herself was anything but deflated. With gorgeous black hair, broad face, and green skin courtesy of her half-orc heritage, she was always picture-perfect in her uniform. This morning was no exception.William and I found her at the station's front desk with a basket of chocolate croissants, a toothy grin, and a terrible pun about "breaking fast."

"You've been scarce lately, Red," she continued as she gestured for us to help ourselves to the pastries. To my surprise, William did. "Dusty told me you got something strange in the mail a few days ago."

Trust Dusty, local handy-gnome and gossip extraordinaire, to go about spreading news I thought was secret. If I hadn't been so worried, I might have laughed aloud.

"So," said the officer, "What've you been hiding?"

"Nothing," I said, simultaneously putting the carousel horse and the note on her desk. At her raised eyebrow, I blushed. "Well, nothing that *I* did, anyway. These showed up a few days ago . . ."

While William steadily munched through the supply of chocolate croissants, I filled Officer Thorn in on everything we knew about the carousel horse—which wasn't a lot. But it was enough for the officer to turn grave.

"You might have thought you were kidding about a ring of bandits," she said with a firm glance at William, "but I've had reports of unusual activity of late. Ambushes on mail-carriers and the like." She moved the basket of pastries to the other side of her desk.

"Where?" I asked, hoping for a clue as to which "old friend" had sent the horse along.

Officer Thorn just shrugged. "On the roads."

"Yes, but—"

"Now, you listen to me, Red." This time her chastising tones fell on me, and I stopped protesting. She went on, "You just keep doing exactly what you'd normally do. Keep your head down, but stay alert. People are bound to figure out that you have the horse now that you've gone all over asking folks about it."

"Are you suggesting," I asked, crossing my arms, "that we use a magical object as bait in luring out some roadside bandits? Making *me* the victim of the next attack?"

"Of course not! You aren't a victim," Officer Thorn stood and rounded her desk, giving me a friendly pat on the back. The gesture felt more like a mossy thunderclap. "You're my unofficial assistant, and I need you back on the force, not lurking in your shop brooding over some toy."

"You just contradicted yourself . . ."

"Don't bother, Red," William piped up. He was still eyeing the chocolate croissants.

"And anyway, I haven't been hiding in my shop," I added, gaining steam. "I had a feeling something like this was bound to happen, and I wanted to find out *why*—"

"That's the spirit," said Officer Thorn. "But put that on the back shelf for now, would you? We don't need any magic interfering here. This is just some good old-fashioned trap-setting."

"Too late," William mumbled. He was probably talking about the magic; either way, I paused for a moment to shush him.

Although I couldn't help pointing out that Officer Thorn hadn't *actually* set any traps.

"Not as far as you know," Officer Thorn retorted with a grin. "Besides, if you ask me, that entire shop of yours is a trap just waiting to happen. I pity the criminal who tries to *croiss-ant* you and your dog."

* * *

William *hates* being referred to simply as a "dog." I don't know if it was that or the worse-than-usual pun, but I pretty much had to drag him out of the station.

"Leave her be," I entreated him through gritted teeth as we lurched into the street. "She's not exactly wrong, and you know it."

"Don't get me started on *you*," William growled back.

"Hey, what's that supposed to mean? I'm just trying to be careful. It's not like we know for sure that anyone else even wants this horse."

"How careful is it to talk about it out on the open road? Especially when sorcerers are coming in from all across Beyond for the big Meeting," William said. He had a point: until that moment, I'd totally forgotten about the Meeting, which was a month-long conference mixed with magical fair, from the sound of it. Sorcerers really were coming from all over for it, as were other magical creatures. I'd never seen the Meeting myself, but it was a local tradition. "You have no idea who could be listening," William added.

"Do you think the Meeting has anything to do with the—"

"Don't even say it," William said, his nose in the air as he trotted along beside me. "You know, you could get the answers yourself instead of running around to everyone else."

I knew from experience where this conversation was headed. Fortunately, we were halfway back to the shop; the back alley was just coming into view on the left, and once we were there I could take refuge in my lab. "Just because I come from Seers doesn't mean that I have any magical aptitude, as you know very well. I'm a *scientist*."

"I'm just saying, if you would do the Seer thing more often then I wouldn't have to worry about you blabbing to the wrong sorcerer or running right into bandits."

"But I don't *do* the 'Seer thing.' Do we really need to have that conversation again, Mother?" I looked away from William, exasperated, and skidded to an instant halt as my eyes caught sight of a shadow. Exasperation turned quickly to incredulity.

Beside me, William vibrated like a twanged bowstring. "Someone's trying to get into the shop."

"I know that," I hissed at him, as though the intruder might hear us all the way out in the road. "I just saw him come around the corner."

William and I blinked at one another. I made my decision.

"What are you doing?" William called as I ran ahead, ducking so that I wasn't visible from the back patio. He broke into a lope to keep up.

"What's it look like? You go get Thorn!"

"While you do what? Offer yourself up to the thief on a silver platter?"

"I'm just going to watch him and see where he goes." When William didn't stop following me to the shop, I added, "The faster you get Thorn, the less time I have to do anything dumb!"

I said it to distract him, of course. I didn't plan to do anything stupid. Who ever does? But William bought it and streaked off in the direction we'd come.

Meanwhile I crept silently into the tiny yard behind my shop. The thought of roadside attacks had been disturbing, of course, as had the nameless dread which had followed me since the carousel horse showed up. But this fool had stepped on *my* turf. I knew exactly where to walk so he wouldn't hear me, and where to stand so he couldn't see.

I took up a post along the fence underneath an overhanging plum tree, behind a ramshackle shed. I could see the man as he glanced furtively around my yard, but when he looked my way all he only saw dappled shadow. I tried to gauge who he might be: pointed ears suggested elven blood, and yet height-wise he looked shorter than my five foot eight. He wore leather armor and carried not one, not two, but a veritable dining room set of daggers.

"Ugh, no, don't, don't," I mumbled, watching him run his hands along the frame and test the latch. The glass was unbreakable; William's ward ensured that. What I worried about was my menagerie of potted plants, all far more valuable than anyone realized, which at any moment the thief might grab and try to toss through the window. The result would be a broken pot, and I had made those all specially—not to mention I'd only just fed all the plants some Fertilizing Powder that took days to properly prepare. The last thing I wanted was for all that time spent grinding down ingredients and letting them cure to go to waste.

Quickly I calculated my options. William had probably made it to Thorn already, but they'd take another few minutes to arrive. Too long for the safety of my plants. I stepped out from my shaded hiding spot, my eyes fixed on the thief. He had his back turned to me.

I bent and grabbed a rock from the scrubby grass and hauled my arm back. After a moment to aim, the missile sailed straight and true into the back of the cretin's head.

"OI!" The man jumped straight up like the patio bit him. He whirled. "You!"

"Nice to meet you too," I said, stepping back into the shadow.

"Missy, you stole a *very* valuable trinket. The Grand Sorcerer wants it back. I could pay you gold—"

I stopped listening and dropped into a crouch, picking up several more rocks. Now yelling in frustration—*good*, I thought, *that'll bring the Officer here even quicker*—the would-be burglar barged right over my biggest pot and launched himself daggers-first in my direction.

I dodged from my corner, easily evading the bandit. As I went I threw a rock that caught his left hand and made him drop his dagger. Though I wasn't a practicing Seer, my heritage blessed me with swift feet and a very sure eye.

"Hey, idiot! Want to tell me what happened to my friend?"

The man's gaze swiveled to me, and I'm sorry to say he smiled. It was revolting. "Ye mean he didn't tell you about them?"

"Sure he did," I lied. "But aren't there two sides to every story? Unless you aren't bright enough to remember what side you're on."

"Ye got quite the mouth for nothing but a shopgirl," the man growled back. "Best hand over the Mariner's Ride before I get impatient."

And then I finally caught on. *Mariner's Ride. The Grand Sorcerer.* I drew breath to make a retort—something very witty, I'm sure, just as soon as I thought of it—but was spared the trouble when a bolt of black flew into the yard, and Officer Thorn's panting face appeared in the alley rapping smartly, "Po-lice!"

Everything went still. In the middle of the yard, two muddy boots stuck out from beneath a glowing dog.

The bandit recovered first. "I want this woman charged with theft and assaul— *oof.*"

William sat more firmly on the man and looked back at Officer Thorn. "I *told* you I wasn't pulling your leg."

* * *

". . . And so, Thorn's got him in her dungeon as we speak," I finished. "Well—it's not a *real* dungeon—though he does deserve one, in my opinion. But the Belville jail is very *like* a dungeon, especially if you're there with Officer Thorn and William at the same time. We can't be sure which 'Grand Sorcerer' he meant, since there's a million of them in town for the Meeting and they all think they're the greatest thing since magitech. But we're not giving up."

I paused, smiling, but still a little uncertain.

Scilis, an adventurer I'd met ages ago in the Dragon Lands on some grand and exciting quest, nodded encouragingly. Tall and scraggly and covered in haphazard plate armor, he looked exactly as he had all those years ago—aside from being a bit see-through.

Yes, Scilis was dead. Just about to cross into the afterlife, in fact. I'd met all kinds of people all across Beyond, but I'd never yet talked to a ghost. The only reason I could talk to one now was something the bandit had said. *The Mariner's Ride.*

That was what Scilis had mentioned in his letter, not some made-up "nole." His *r* had blended into his *i,* and the *d* came apart into an *o* and an *l.* In talking it over, William and I had agreed that this was the magic inside the horse, the spell he hadn't been able to see because it didn't represent a *thing* exactly. It wasn't a *what,* or even a *how,* but a *how to get there.*

Acting on a hunch and under William's careful supervision, I'd clutched the tiny horse, asked to find its most recent owner, and been pulled—like a buggy behind a very excitable pony—to a sycamore perched on the hillside overlooking town. And now I sat against its trunk, talking to someone beyond the grave. Someone, I realized now, who had been trailing along behind me ever since the carousel horse showed up: that feeling of foreboding heightened, then vanished when I looked at Scilis' familiar face.

The breeze ruffled through the leaves above. I still clutched the carousel horse in my hand. As long as I held it, the world shimmered blue and silver, as though the earth was weightless gauze and life itself had put on twilight glasses. But I had a feeling that as soon as I let go of the horse, the spell would be broken. I'd see the light of sunset, and feel heavy again, and smell the hearths from town. And I wouldn't see Scilis any more. This was my chance.

"There's no need to worry, you know. Everything's safe," I promised. William had devised a special arcane box in which to keep the precious carousel horse hidden, but I didn't want to say that aloud on the hilltop just in case.

Scilis nodded again, as though this was exactly what he had planned. It seemed that, even though I could see him in this strange place where our world and the next overlapped, he couldn't speak. In the blue light, William's words about *ghost ships* came back to me.

"I . . . I'm sorry," I said, on impulse. "Where I come from, everyone likes to say that things happen for a reason. But I've always been on the fence about fate, myself."

Scilis shook his head this time, and beamed at me—the smile of an adventurer off on a new journey. He waved his arms expansively down the hill, as if saying, *go, enjoy!*

I laughed. I stretched out my legs in front of me, attempted to touch my toes—I've never been able to, but every once in a while I like to check—and stood. "Alright, I'm going. This has been—crazy, but I'm glad I got to see you again. Are you going, too? No more lingering around?"

Scilis nodded one more time. And he waved. Around him, the air seemed wispier than ever.

"Okay, then," I whispered, smiling. "Good luck."

I didn't say goodbye, not exactly. In Beyond, life can take you to unexpected places. And although I'd never been too sure about the future being fated, Scilis's trust showed me that my past really had stayed with me, just below the surface.

And that carousel horse was only the beginning.

2

A Red Storm

The Second Carousel Caper

The storm hit Belville out of nowhere. Its howling winds and lashing rain drove before them a pitiful, battered paper kite with an invitation for me tied in its trailing string.

This was not a normal occurrence for sleepy, pastoral Belville. I could tell from the start that someone either wanted to give me something I didn't want, or to hide themselves, or both. And my companion, a shaggy black dog-shaped familiar who went by the name William, was having none of it.

"I'm just saying," said he, as he remained firmly on the cushions in my tiny apartment's bay window. (He insisted he didn't mind storms, but as long as there was thunder rolling, he rarely left his comfort zone.) "It took magic to get that thing to *your* shop's front door. Whoever sent it might be behind the storm itself. Come on, Red, who in this town would go to such trouble to send you love notes? We've barely been here a season."

"So? A season's long enough if it's love at first sight," I teased him. I'm too much of a rover to believe in all-consuming love like that: I guess I've always had other goals, opening my very own alchemy and potions shop being one. "Cool it, Mother, it's not a love note. In fact, I'll read it to you. It say—"

"Don't," William interrupted, his gruff voice bark-like enough that I realized he really was upset. He's told me over and over that I shouldn't read anything that might be a spell aloud, but arcane details like that go in one ear and out the other for me. That's one of the reasons it's handy to keep William around. Even if he can be a grouch.

I shrugged. As soon as I'd closed the shop that day I'd brought the kite and the curious invitation up to the apartment, and now all three items—myself included, because in the simple act of opening the front door to catch the kite, I'd been drenched—were dripping all over the trunk at the end of my bed. No big deal: I'd waterproofed it, storm-proofed it, even deluge-proofed it long ago. From my seat atop my trusty luggage, I leaned over and handed William the paper. In my mind, I ran over what he would read:

To Miss Red, Alchemist and Amateur Sleuth:

You are cordially invited to a dinner party at Sunset House in two days' time. We invite all our guests to arrive when they are done with business for the day, and wear whatever they're most comfortable in.

You may be interested to know that Sunset House is not floored with gold, as rumors may have led you to believe, but is home to a much more valuable substance. And if you prove strong enough, you may leave with not one but two gifts.

We regret that we are unable to accept extras or substitutions for our guests.

"*Gifts?*" William snorted.

"Well? It isn't bewitched, is it?" I asked this only because I was quite certain it was just average paper, written upon by an old-fashioned hand. As William furrowed furry eyebrows, I grinned and added, "Seems polite and straightforward to me. Though I don't see why they had to add the bit about 'amateur sleuth.'"

"Probably whoever sent it is friends with Officer Thorn," growled William. Our local police officer, an impressive and impulsive half-orc, had decided within our first days of arrival in Belville that I would make an excellent "unofficial partner." "Whatever they've got is probably evidence."

"It's possible." My last encounter with Thorn had only been a few days ago, but I wouldn't have called it "sleuthing;" it had begun with the arrival of a strange carousel horse statuette and ended with a trip into the twilight land of ghosts. "What's the deal with Sunset House, anyway? I haven't heard of it."

"That's because you spend too much time mixing potions and not enough time listening."

"Oh, you mean, doing my job, which keeps this roof over our heads?"

Rain splattered on the wavy glass behind William. He shook his head at it, and at my grin. "*Everyone* in Belville knows about Sunset House. It's cut into the hillside at the western edge of town, across Market Square from us. Dusty says not just the floors but everything in there's gilded—though I guess this guy'd say different."

"Yeah." I set my elbow on my knees and my chin in my hand, musing. "A substance more valuable, huh? It could be any number of things. If the house is in a hillside, it could be on a vein—"

"Red!" William snapped. "Tell me you recognize this as an obvious appeal to your weird, mad-scientist reputation. He's trying to overrule your better judg—"

"I have a reputation as a mad scientist?" I chuckled as I pushed back my ever-present alchemists' goggles—goggles which, I suppose, had helped cement said reputation. To me they were just practical, not least because they kept back my long black hair. Still, I was no stranger to being stereotyped, and as far as stereotypes go, 'mad scientist' wasn't too bad.

"*Red . . .*"

"You're just jealous," I told William, standing. "I'm going, and that's final. Now, I'm going to go dry off, and then we can think about dinner."

* * *

I was dismissive of love earlier, but the truth is, I love many things—adventure included. I grew up in a nomadic culture: it's in the roots of my soul. And while I knew what I was doing when I chose to settle in Belville and open a shop, it *was* a change of pace. From fast-as-you-can to zero, you might say. Aside from the odd crime-solving assignment, life had become routine, and if I'm honest, I decided to go to Sunset House for the pure newness of it.

I was at Sunset House precisely at sundown, dressed in my most respectable tunic and tights, invitation in hand and eyes

22

wide open for new discoveries.

"Welcome, Miss Red," a voice began as the huge, ornate doors opened. The house itself wasn't ostentatious: large and blocky, sure, but in a homey and intriguing kind of way—not at all the haunted mansion William had led me to expect. And the sprite that greeted me was all sparkle and wind, the least spooky ghost imaginable.

"Everyone is in the Dawn Room," the little swirl of colored air informed me. "Master Jack wishes you to feel at home."

Wondering who "Master Jack" might be, I followed the wind sprite through the darkened hall to what could only be the Dawn Room. The light from the glowing fireplace illuminated gilded surfaces everywhere. What wasn't gilded was draped in woven blankets of orange, red, and yellow. On pillows and chaises around the room, I saw half a dozen people lounging. An elderly woman chatted with a middle-aged, clearly fae woman who shone around the edges and could only be the lady of the house; what looked like a snake trying to balance on its tail huddled gloomily in one corner; a robed figure ignored all of us to peruse the bookshelf set into one wall; and a very handsome, copper-skinned man leaned upon the fireplace.

"Welcome, welcome, Red!" The man at the fireplace moved to shake my hand. "I'm Jack—just Jack, please, we're not stuffy here. And across the room you'll see my sister, Miss Potter. I've convinced her to open up the house for a little harmless entertainment."

'Harmless,' in my experience, is a word only applied to dangerous things. But it was hard to be suspicious of Jack; his light brown eyes crinkled when he smiled, and he leaned toward me like a friend. He smelled like campfire smoke and sweet grasses.

"Well, you certainly have an interesting range of guests," I said, returning his grin.

"Don't we? And here's one I believe you've met, currently trying to lighten my sister's bookshelves. Oh, Luca!"

"I would never steal anything!" The man in scholar's robes came hurrying over to us. I'd met him in the bookstore several times. Though his hood obscured his hair, he seemed to have less dust about him than usual. "I was only interested in reading them."

"Even worse," said Jack cheerfully. To me, he added, "Keep an eye on the lad for me, will you? We meant to invite his senior, the delightful old man called Owl; you've met him, of course. But lo and behold, this vagabond turned up instead."

"Owl couldn't come," protested Luca. "Shop business."

I turned to Jack with an eyebrow raised. "I thought the rule was 'no extras or substitutions.'"

"And if it wasn't, you'd have brought your furry sidekick?" Jack ran a hand through his long, mussed hair and grinned. "Much fun as that would have been, I'm afraid you're right. The rules are the rules, and that's why I'm asking you to look after our little party-crasher for me."

At that point as if on cue Miss Potter called, and Jack strode jauntily away. I turned abruptly to Luca, my frown returning.

"What *are* you doing here?"

"Hello to you, too, Red," he said sullenly. "I told you, Owl sent me. He doesn't like to go out."

"So I've gathered. But couldn't you at least have thought about something other than books for two seconds?"

Luca shuffled. "I *was* talking to Miss Potter before you got here, but then this Jack guy who knows everything said something about magic objects that rang a bell, and just now when I was looking at their shelves I realized—"

"Officer Thorn reporting!" A brash, happy voice strode into the room.

"Our final guest has arrived," the sparkling sprite clarified uselessly in the wake of the police officer, who fit into the room like it was half a size too small.

"One doesn't 'report' to a dinner party, dear," said Jack, leaping to take Thorn's hand. He smiled and gestured to all of us as he said, "One is welcomed."

* * *

Dinner went exactly as could be expected. We were shepherded to a grand, round table set with colorful dishes. I ended up sandwiched between Luca and the elderly lady, who introduced herself as Cairn.

"As in, a way-marker for a trail?" I asked, to be sure I'd heard her right.

"That's it." She cocked her head and grinned at me as the soup made it round the table. "I did a bit of traveling in my youth, for my shop. I'm an antiques dealer, did I say that? Ah, well, now you know it all the better. My friends used to tease me for being ubiquitous. 'When we see you in town, we know we've made it to the right place,' they'd say. A traveling merchant knows many things, isn't that so, Miss Alchemist?"

"Please, just Red is fine." I laughed and chatted with Cairn throughout the first course, successfully ignoring both Luca beside me and Thorn across from me—and that was a feat, because she was as loud as a bull in a music shop. Just as the main course arrived and I was about to try an ornate savory pie called Trickster's Delight—so named because it's made to look like one thing and taste like another—Luca served up a sharp elbow to my ribs.

"Ow! What was that for?"

"You're supposed to be watching me," he replied matter-of-factly, like he hadn't just resorted to violence at the most upscale party Belville had ever seen.

"Well, I sure am now," I muttered as I picked up my fork.

"Good. Then you can catch me when listening to another moment of Ryuko's withering conversation drains me of the will to live."

"Luca!" I reproached. The man had fine—if overly casual—manners in the bookstore; I'd never pegged him for the type to be wantonly rude at dinner.

"Oh don't worry, Ryuko doesn't mind. Do you? See, no, he doesn't. I think he's quite pleased about it, actually."

I peered around Luca at this "Ryuko," who turned out to be the snake-like figure I'd seen earlier. Even at a gaily candle-lit table, he managed to sink into shadow. I realized that, although scales were present, he was mostly human. Only a human could look so gloomy.

"Red! Luca! What are you two plotting?" Officer Thorn barked across the table.

I bit back the first thing that came to mind, which was along the lines of *why are you here again?* and in the silence Luca beat me to responding.

"Are you here on a case, Officer Thorn?"

"A case! Of course not." It was Miss Potter who replied. I turned to look at her again. The fae blood made her glowing features a little difficult to look at; it was like trying to pin down leaf shadows in the breeze. She was smiling almost as though she had a secret as she turned to her brother. "At least, not yet. Isn't that right, Jack?"

Jack's answer was a wide grin. "Let's not ruin the fun, shall we?"

Conversation blossomed once more—and there was Luca at my shoulder again. "Why do you think they really invited us all? It's a weird group, don't you think?"

"Even weirder when you think it was *Owl* they actually invited," I noted, looking around the table again. A police officer, an antiques dealer, an alchemist, a scholarly bookstore clerk, and a whatever-Ryuko-was. Judging by his behavior, something semi-legal at best. I could think of nothing that was common between all of us. "Did Owl's invitation say anything about gifts?"

Luca's fork paused on its way to his mouth. "Other than awesome food?" he grinned. "What else could you want?"

"Nothing, and that's what I'm worried about," I joked, though a hint of foreboding tickled my spine. "All I want right now is to be so full I end up rolling home."

* * *

"I'm sure you're all wondering why we invited you here," said Jack later. The sky peaking down through the skylights was dark, and we'd just finished a lovely dessert of something smothered in syrup and cream—wine had been flowing freely, and with Luca bothering one ear and Cairn pouring stories into the other, I hadn't had much chance to examine the food. "The answer is, it gets tiring, always eating at that big table without a crowd!"

The crowd in question was gathered in what Miss Potter called the "waiting room." The floor was a pearlescent tile and the walls hosted expertly done murals, each depicting what seemed to be the same man riding variously colored horses. There were chairs of all shapes and descriptions scattered around, many inlaid with jewels; in these we lunged, and indulgently we laughed at Jack's joke.

"But since you're here," Jack added, "let's play a game."

Game? Like when he'd said "harmless" earlier, the word did not sound right. I struggled into an upright position.

"I propose a scavenger hunt. What for, you ask? Well, that's a secret. But I promise you," and here I swear he looked directly into my soul, "that you'll want it. It's hidden somewhere in this house. To help you find it, we'll give you clues—four clues. And four rules."

Jack paused and looked around. Like a teacher who'd mentioned extra credit to a handful of high achievers, he had everyone's attention. "Very good, then. The clues are:

"The object you're looking for represents one of five. It is in wait above, hidden well. It's a heavy burden to carry, and it's made of red shell.

"Now before you rush off, the rules. You may work together, but there will be no stealing. And no violence, please. And just to make things interesting . . . there can be no more than two people in a room at a time. If you think you know what it is, you can't say anything until you find it."

Wait, we can work together, but not all together, and we can't talk about it? I blinked. My food coma had vanished as fast as a jackalope across open plains. But even though my mind raced, I didn't voice my questions: Jack's smile brooked no argument.

"Well, then, what are you waiting for?" He beamed. "First one to find it, bring it back here to Miss Potter and she'll tell you what you've won. If nothing else, it's the perfect opportunity to explore, eh?"

"This sort of thing's right up your alley, isn't it, Red?" Officer Thorn boomed from the corner. "Well just you wait. I'll give you a run for your money!"

She strode out of the room before I could reply. I paused, amused that of all of us it was apparently Thorn and Cairn, who was already on her feet and examining the ceilings, who were most intrigued. Looking around, I saw Ryuko oozing out the side door. *Okay, I guess everyone is taking this seriously,* I realized.

When I looked up, Jack was grinning at me. Discreetly, with his hand at his waist as though maybe he was adjusting his loose shirt, he pointed into the main hall.

As my head swiveled where he directed, my gaze finding nothing out of the ordinary, Luca popped up beside me. "What do you think it is?"

"Oh, I see you've opted for 'working together,'" I observed, wondering if I dared follow Jack's suggestion. Would that be cheating? It'd only be cheating if he was actually telling me something useful . . .

Luca, meanwhile, shrugged. The gesture made his hood shift, and his green eyes glinted against his dark skin. "Well, Officer Thorn beat me to making it a competition, and I'm too competitive to do something someone else already did. What do you say?"

"I say . . ." I hesitated, then decided. Jack was right: this was, if nothing else, a chance to explore. Maybe the mystery object of our hunt was that "valuable substance" my invitation had mentioned. "We haven't seen all the rooms on this floor, much less in the house."

"Right, so, mapping time." Luca fell into step behind me as I stalked into the main hall. I'd made it past the kitchen (huge enough to make an amateur cook like me drool), back through the dining room, and into the Dawn Room again before I realized that Luca had pulled a journal and pencil out of his voluminous robes and was literally *mapping* our progress.

I stopped short, distracted. "What are you doing? Does Owl make you carry those things around all the time?"

"I do have some good ideas myself, you know," Luca returned. "Owl never writes anything down. This is all me. See? I figure we can go back and put a cross through rooms we've searched properly."

His drawing, which he thrust out to me as he spoke, was not bad. It was an easy house to draw: the whole footprint was one big rectangle with a large central hall and three rooms lined up on either side. He'd labeled each room and even added a hasty suggestion of the furniture inside.

This clerk had it all figured out. I crossed my arms. "Is that so?"

"Yeah. Now come on, there's still two rooms aside from the Waiting Room to do, and I can hear the Officer searching up a storm across the hall already!"

You can? I could only hear a low scuffling, and my hearing was better than average. Still, setting aside my incredulity, I followed Luca into the room across the hall.

The room we found might have been called a "breakfast room" by someone proper like Cairn—or our hostess, for that matter. It took up the front corner of the house, bordering the waiting room. Chairs and a small table had been arranged beside a large window, while at the back of the room a few musical instruments stood in front of artfully cluttered shelves. The clutter actually looked to be art itself, little watercolors and pottery pieces. I couldn't see too well, on account of Officer Thorn tromping up and down along the length of the wall, lifting up every single artifact and setting it back down with something less than precision.

"What are you doing?" I asked Thorn pleasantly.

"Go away, Red. No more'n two to a room, don't you remember?"

Much as it was music to my ears to hear Officer Thorn tell me to go away instead of dragging me into some scheme, I was a little miffed. Looking to my right, I saw I'd missed Ryuko's presence: he was in a corner, studying the curtain rods. Before I could speak, Luca tugged at my sleeve from the doorway.

"One more room!" Luca chirped, towing me toward the back of the house. Over his shoulder he yelled, "Remember, officer, no violence!"

"No rule-breaking!" she hollered back.

"That includes violence against the collections!" Luca shouted, his voice echoing in the hallway. "Or it should, anyway," he added to me.

"It *should* include no violence against everyone's eardrums," I protested lightly. "Did you have to get her into a shouting match?"

"Oh come on, Red. It's just a g—"

Luca's voice died and his knees buckled as we turned the corner into the final room. He swayed like a swooning maiden.

"I am *not* going to catch you," I warned him.

"It's a . . . It's a *library*," he breathed.

I rolled my eyes. "What tipped you off? The massive amount

of books, or . . ." The sentence trailed off as I wandered into the center of the darkened room. What had been a joke was overtaken by wonder as I crouched in front of a small round dais supporting a beautiful fire grate. "Or the extremely rare Ever-Burning Coals?"

"I get it," Luca said, grinning as he looked around at walls lined with shelves and a ring of chairs around the fire that had taken my breath away. "Because stories are something you share around a fire, right? That's where they came from. This is *awesome!*"

"Isn't it?" I hadn't heard any footsteps, but Jack was in our midst, grinning as he gestured expansively. "Could the red shell enigma you seek be hidden amongst the books, you think? Or perhaps among the alchemical wonders Miss Red so aptly identified?"

"I've never seen specimens burning so well," I said, hoping the shadow obscured the fact that I blushed at the flattery. "That glow is fantastic! How do you do it?"

Jack cocked his head, smiling. "Is that really what you want to know, Red?"

I hesitated: he was using his "harmless" voice. Jack turned so he was facing Luca, too. "I'm letting everyone ask me one question about the secret object."

Luca's mouth flattened. "How do we know we can trust your answer?"

Jack put his hands in his pockets. "Well, if you don't trust the person who set up the game you're playing, then you need more help than I can give you, don't you?"

"What kind of red shell?"

The question was out of my mouth before I could think better of it, and I could tell from Luca's glance that he didn't think it was a very good one. In fact he went so far as to put his hand to his forehead and let out an exasperated sigh.

Jack focused on me, his eyes twinkling. "You're thinking to yourself, shells don't truly have color, do they? The color comes from impurities inside. You're clever, aren't you, Miss Alchemist? On its own, you might know the material as nacre."

"Great," said Luca dryly.

I shot him a look. "Nacre isn't that heavy."

"So?"

Just as I was debating whether to explain to my self-appointed associate that *heaviness* had been one of our clues and must therefore refer to some metaphysical burden, probably to do with the object's shape or nature, and as such it was probably some bit of meaningful art that *wouldn't* be hiding amongst his precious books, I realized that it was difficult to glare at him because the air in the room had turned smoky.

I turned to look down at the embers, distracted. But they were fine. Better than fine, actually.

"Oh, my," said Jack, looking at the gray clouds above us like he was searching for shapes to point out. "You know, Officer Thorn asked about the material of the mystery object, too. Ryuko, on the other hand, asked about a method of seeing it amid all the other objects in the house." He shrugged and added, "I might have told him that inhaling burning sage would help."

Luca waved a hand through thickening air. "You invited a party guest to burn your house down?"

"The house will be fine," Jack said confidently.

"We might not be if we don't get some fresh air," I decided. "Come on, it might be better in the hallway. Hasn't anyone thought to open a window?" Still muttering to myself and mulling over Jack's clues, I led the charge into the two-story hall. Luca was muttering something too—along the lines of *"but this is the direction the smoke is coming from,"* or something equally silly—and Jack seemed to be whistling. Over them both and over the increased noise of footsteps racing through the house, I heard Officer Thorn saying, "Young man, proper procedure would be to light one bundle at a time."

"Just one didn't work," Ryuko hissed back. Through the fog, he seemed to have a dozen bunches of herbs sticking from his arms and piles around his feet, most of them smoking healthily. Clearly, Ryuko was not one who believed in doing things by halves.

Officer Thorn saw us coming and called, "Hey! Does the hallway count as a room?"

I sighed and ended up coughing. "Is now really the time, Thorn?"

"Every good assistant should know it's always time for rules!"

"Not your assistant," I mumbled, ducking to avoid the smoke. "Can't we open the front door?"

"And risk letting just *anyone* inside?" Thorn stiffened and something whizzed over her head, disappearing into the smoke. Several dull *thuds* followed as it hit a wall and slid to the floor.

"Looks like there's already strange things inside," Luca said. "Anyone seen Cairn?"

"I might have," said Jack, who seemed to be observing his nails as another lasso-shaped shadow passed over his shoulder, "informed her that 'waiting above' in fact referred to something that could obscure itself as mist."

I wheeled on our host. Beautiful and alluring he might be,

but I can't *stand* being messed with and I was already hanging on to the end of my rope by a pinkie finger and a prayer. I was about to read him the riot act regarding inviting people over and then making them run all over a house like ninnies with nets and torches—but my eye caught on something above his head.

It wasn't in the smoke. *That* idea was about as idiotic as the idea that sage was going to give anyone X-ray vision. Over Jack's head I could see through the doorway into the waiting room, where Miss Potter sat placidly, toying with something in her lap. And above *her* head, I could see a lip cut into the wall. It blended into the mural, obscured by the image of a setting sun.

"I'd hate to think a little smoke could deter an alchemist," Jack said to me, grinning. "You look displeased. Are you going to make us all evacuate?"

There was something in his voice, a hint that choosing not to play his game would have real-life consequences. And on top of that he was looking at me like somehow to be reasonable was to be cowardly in this situation.

I was *not* a coward. I gritted my teeth and pushed past him into the waiting room.

* * *

"Red!" Miss Potter looked up from the fabric in her lap, and she smiled as I entered the room. "I have so looked forward to meeting you."

"Oh—thanks." I paused at the center of the room, struck by awkwardness. *What do I say? 'Nice of you to be nice to me, can I ransack your walls so we can get this game over with?'* "You and your brother, uh, sure seem to know a lot."

"And that surprises you?" Miss Potter tilted her head, much as Jack had done earlier. Her face still looked blurry, like many artists had each painted versions of it one on top of the other, but it was also undeniably lovely and wise. "Go on, child."

"Well really, I'm not that—" I bit my tongue. Arguing with my hostess seemed even ruder than climbing a wall in her home, so I stuck with the latter option and did as she said.

I'm reasonably tall, for a human at least, and I wasn't about to shift furniture around so I could get my boots all over it. So instead of pulling a chair over to the hidden ledge I'd noticed from the hallway, I reached up blindly and groped. This is never a good idea. All kinds of nasties "wait above," including but not limited to poky things, spiders, and dust animated by the passage of time. But I was pretty certain that I would find what I was looking for. It seemed very much like Jack to send everyone out looking for a thing that had been right in front of their eyes at the start.

My hand hit an object—a surprisingly large one. I reached up to fish it out of the alcove sunk into the wall, mentally reviewing everything Jack had said: *red nacre, one of five, heavy weight, probably emotional or magic . . .*

My heart jolted. I could hear William saying *"There's a charm I can't see on the inside,"* as if I was back at the kitchen table examining a cursed carousel horse statuette again. That statue had cost a friend his life. *What if there are more?*

When my hands lowered and I realized I was holding a basket, not a horse, I breathed a sigh of relief.

"Congratulations, Red," Miss Potter said, slowly standing as I faced her. "I wanted you to have it from the beginning. But to guard them, you must be clever, determined, and brave, just as you have proven yourself to be tonight."

My thoughts turned desperate. *She might have any number of things she wanted me to have . . . right?*

I groaned. "Tell me it's not . . ."

Miss Potter smiled. "Look inside."

Like a free-range toddler told to open a box of soap, I did, probably curling my lip and scrunching my nose. There inside the basket nestled a small, beautifully carved, pearly red carousel horse.

"Jack said it was something I would want," I pointed out, going from recalcitrant toddler to angsty teen in the blink of an eye. It wasn't what my better self would have done, but my better self was in a corner having a panic attack about becoming guardian to yet another cursed relic.

"You will," Miss Potter said gently. "You've had a long night, Red. It is time you took your prize and made your way home."

* * *

In my dream both Jack and Miss Potter rode horses, and so did the man from the murals. I looked down at the carousel horse in my hand: one of five.

Feel like a storm is coming? Jack grinned. *When all the horses come together, the world as you know it will be ruined.*

There are others looking for them. Do not carry the burden alone, Miss Potter warned. *This is something you must do together . . .*

"What, by all the moons and the stars, is wrong with you, Red?"

William's voice shook me awake. Sunlight attacked my eyes.

All my blankets were on the floor.

"First you come in practically in the middle of the night, acting like a zombie and mumbling about protection. Then you spend all night thrashing from one side of your bed to another and finally when I'm forced to give up sleeping I get up and I find *this*!"

I sat up, my hands over my face as I tried to ascertain what he was talking about with the minimal amount of eye-opening required. "What time is it?"

"What. Is. This," William said.

That didn't strike me as much of an answer, so I removed my hands and looked around for my own clues. I still wore my party clothes; William stood with his front paws on my trunk, his eyes glowing; and judging by the angle of the light on the windows, it was mid-day.

My gaze fell to the leaping red carousel horse, on its side on said trunk. "Good thing nacre is pretty sturdy, I guess."

"I *said*—"

"William, you know what it is." I yawned, and my many houseplants waved in answer. "They gave it to me, the people at Sunset House. And before you say anything, yes, I made it plain that I did not want it. But they insisted."

I paused, thinking of what Miss Potter had said. *You will.*

William shuffled, unappeased. "Tell me everything. Do you realize what this is? It's one of the five horses the sun god uses to ride across the sky. It's associated with *storms*. This is what caused all that wind and rain and that cursed kite!"

"No, I didn't know that. I guess that's why they didn't want you there," I yawned again. "You would have spoiled the 'fun.'"

Groggily, I explained everything that I remembered. It took a while for the tale to get out—not only because my brain moved slowly, but because William kept interrupting. By the end of it, he sprawled next to me on top of jumbled sheets and together we contemplated the statuette.

"Think they'll really 'ruin the world?'," I asked, dryly. When William said nothing, I added, "At least you already made a magical safe for keeping them in."

William snorted. "How many are there?"

"Dunno. Jack said something about five, but I think that was more about the painting . . ." I waved my hand. A chill washed over me as I once again heard dream-Jack saying, *there's more.*

"Yeah, the horses of the sun god. Jeez, she really put some kind of sleeping spell on you, didn't she?"

I scratched my head, setting aside foreboding thoughts, and wondered if I should think about breakfast, or lunch. "You're the one who can see those things."

"Whatever she did to you is more like a glow, not a charm like what's in these." William put his head on his paws, looking back at the horse. Apparently its charm was greater than the potential that I'd been magicked.

This time, it was my turn to snort. "Why'd they go to all that effort? Is that the kind of trouble it takes to get rid of those statues?"

"Don't you ever listen, Red? She said she wanted to test you first. And your invitation said—" William's head lifted once more, his black eyes fixed on me. "Tell me again who was there, and what they said to you in the dream?"

"Something about other people looking for the horses, and not to carry it alone. Me, Luca, Officer Thorn, Cairn—the antiques lady—and some guy named Ryuko."

William chuckled. "Miss Potter didn't just give you a horse, Red. She gave you a council of war."

"Ugh," was all I said.

Could there be anything worse than a war you never wanted in the first place?

Still, as I washed up and began moving, my reluctance faded into acceptance. *So there's more of these horses out there,* I thought. *More mythical beings, more little charms.* I'd never been a collector myself, but it was clear these carousel statues were important. And even though it seemed like an awful lot of trouble . . .

. . . at least now I knew I'd have a party of people I might turn to for help.

3

An Iron Voice

The Third Carousel Caper

Before I took my place at the head of the kitchen table, I grabbed a handful of the double-chocolate cookies I'd just made. Cocoa was going to be essential if I had to take part in, much less *lead*, a Council of War.

That's what William, magical black dog extraordinaire, had taken to calling this eclectic group: my "Council of War," capital letters and all. I wasn't sold on the idea, particularly because I hadn't even met some of its members until an unfortunate dinner party hosted by a trickster several days before. And because I didn't see why collecting charmed carousel horse statuettes should count as "war." Especially when I didn't want the dratted things in the first place. I prefer knick knacks that come in shapes which can hold plants—and which *don't* hold mysterious powers.

But because I'd learned from experience that the last thing I could do in small-town Belville was run my alchemy shop in peace, and more importantly because one of my friends had given his life for those carousel horses, I resigned myself to an evening of very strange conversation.

"Alright, everyone," I began. To be honest it was more a sigh than a call to order. "I'm guessing we need to start at the beginning with the 'tiny magic horse' talk, right?"

William sneezed, as though allergic to my reluctance. Since there were five of us crowded around my little dining room table, squeezed into the apartment above my shop, his dog breath managed to reach every person present. As we cringed, he looked up grinning. "Everyone knows already, Red."

I focused on the important matters first. "Stop panting, will you? Or maybe eat a cookie. What do you mean, everyone knows?"

Luca, a clerk at the local bookstore who was never to be parted from his scholar's robes and his impulse to help, pushed a cookie in William's direction while William cocked his furry ears at me and said smugly, "I keep *telling* you you should pay more attention to town gossip."

"The dog's right," said Officer Thorn. A half-orc police-woman, she sat across the table from William, which was for the best. The two were often at each other's throats, but I doubted it was due to actual animosity. It seemed almost like a shared language.

"Not a dog," William muttered.

"Everyone knows about the game at the dinner party, and how you won a little red horse trinket that brings on storms, and that if you find more of them they could destroy the world," Thorn continued as though blissfully unaware of William's glowering existence. At her elbow Cairn, a nice little old lady who ran an antiques shop, and Ryuko, a scaly and perpetually gloomy probable-delinquent, nodded. "So, out to find them, are you?"

I'd picked the wrong time to eat. My mouth was too full of cookie to contradict her, and in the silence everyone leapt to their own conclusions.

Luca brightened. "I found some really interesting passages in one of the books at the store—"

"Seems to me that they find her," William growled.

"I'm more interested in knowing who else might be looking," said Cairn.

"Too bad you can't make *them* talk," Ryuko observed with a little too much menace.

"I'm not interested in what they have to say," I announced, having finally swallowed my cookie. The cocoa was ashes in my mouth. "And I really don't want any more of them. But . . ."

"But," said Thorn, unexpectedly gently, "we can hardly let these things fall into the wrong hands, can we?"

What else could I do? I gave in. "Right. Fine. So, since we're all agreed . . . Does anyone know anything about them? How many of them there are, where they are, anything like that?"

There was a thoughtful silence across the table. I would have figured Luca'd be the first to volunteer information, but he seemed preoccupied, and in the waiting period Ryuko lifted one pointy-nailed finger. "I didn't agree."

I pursed my lips at him. He was definitely snake-kin—that is, descended from a human tribe with snake characteristics—and while I hate to cast anyone as a villain, he made it a little too easy. On top of his attitude, he was covered in a pattern of purple and black scales and seemed to always be wearing a hood. To be honest, Luca was always wearing a hood too, but Luca had none of the sinewy sense of being just about to strike that Ryuko had. "Remind me," I said dryly, "what is it that you actually do, Ryuko?"

He shifted, his shoulders moving fluidly as he glanced at Officer Thorn. Even though he was taller than her, he probably weighed half as much as she did—and she had the law on her side. "I'm helping out at Priya's curiosity shop, since her other assistant went AWOL."

Cairn looked surprised. "Beth is missing?"

"Not missing," Officer Thorn corrected. "Just unreliable, ever since she started looking into genealogy. Work's not as compelling as history, apparently."

"Whereas, you *are* reliable," William concluded with a hint of irony as he, too, stared down Ryuko.

Ryuko shrugged.

"You don't have to be here if you don't want to," I told him. Ryuko finally met my eyes, and grinned just a little, showing one fang. The expression made him look older than I'd thought he was.

"You don't get a choice," he pointed out. "I'm thinking since I was involved in that party, I don't get one either."

"Alright, then, *now* we're agreed." Once more I looked around the table. "So, anyone have anything they'd like to share?"

"Oh!" Luca broke into the conversation like he'd just woken up. "I wanted to tell you, I found this book. It doesn't actually say anything about carousel horses, but it does talk about charmed objects being bound together in sets, often of nine or twelve, and goes on further to say..."

I lifted an eyebrow at William, who stuck his tongue out

at me. *We're going to be here a long time,* I realized. I grabbed another cookie.

* * *

The Council of War did indeed take a long time, long enough that it was considerably after sunrise when I woke up the next day. I am a morning person usually—by force of habit, if nothing else—but all the dead ends from the night before had me groggy. That, or maybe all the cookies I'd eaten.

As such when the bell at my shop door rang and my first customer for the day walked in, it took me a long moment to realize that it wasn't a customer in search of potions at all. In fact, it was Cairn. And she was even more disheveled and frowny than I was.

"Cairn! What's wrong?" I hastened to pour her some of the tea I liked to keep on hand for guests. William was still snoring upstairs and no one else had come in yet, so we had the shop to ourselves.

"Someone broke into my shop," she told me, her eyes momentarily wavering with tears. "Early this morning. If only I'd stayed the night in town after our meeting! They broke—so many things, Red. Priceless antiques, gone."

"That's awful. I can't imagine anyone doing that here," I said, and meant it. My alchemy shop was my dream come true; I'd be heartbroken if anything happened to it. Heartbroken, and very angry. "How can I help?"

"I've already called Officer Thorn, and she's been over the place. Dusty is helping me clean up. I just don't know anyone who would do such a thing, and told the Officer so. I've had my disagreements with people in town, of course, Priya among them, but theft is no way to solve neighborly differences!"

"It *is* pretty incredible," I agreed. "Was much taken?"

"So far it looks like they didn't steal much—they just smashed through everything . . . like they were looking for something. But they left my safe alone. I've never—I mean, I've had people break into my shop before, of course, though never in Belville. When I was doing roving antiquities and fairs, I saw this kind of thing a lot. But now . . . It's strange. Officer Thorn's going to bring in the town Witch later, see if any spellwork can help."

"And in the meantime, you will recover," I pointed out gently. Cairn's tears had already faded: truly, the woman was every bit as resilient as her stories suggested.

"I wondered—when you get a moment—there's something I want you to look at." When I hesitated, thinking this sounded an awful lot like I was being pulled into another unofficial investigation, she added, "Officer Thorn thought it was a good idea for you to see."

I did see. If Thorn was asking for me, it didn't bode well for my peace and quiet. But because I respected Cairn and really did want to help, I agreed. At the end of my day I packed up some potions and tools, figuring I'd be testing some leftover trace or helping Officer Thorn track down the burglars.

What I *didn't* figure was that I'd be standing in the half-cleaned ruins of Cairn's shop, police spells on the door behind me and Cairn herself with one hand on a broom and the other on her hip, both of us staring at a small carousel horse on the counter.

"We found it there," said Cairn, gesturing through an open doorway into her stockroom. Like the rest of the store, it gave the impression of being tidy and full of interesting things when not ransacked. Cairn had cleaned the front half of her store first, and I saw shards of broken pottery and strings of spilled beads scattered on the floor where she pointed. "It was in a vase. I—I never knew I had them. I don't see how anyone could have known."

"Had *them*?" I asked, though I could tell the idea that one of her treasures had harbored a secret troubled Cairn. She ran her hands through her short gray hair.

"It was a two-part vase—an upper and a lower compartment. I guess you could say there was a third part, too, for the flower. I knew that the flower bit didn't go all the way down, of course, but I thought it was just a fault of the construction. The vase was old, probably as much as a century. I didn't realize—this was hiding in there the entire time."

"And I guess your robbers didn't realize that either?" My stomach turned. What if the statuette was what they had been looking for?

"Actually . . . there were *two* hidden compartments, like I said. One had been smashed open, but while we were looking through the—looking at everything, Officer Thorn happened to step on the base of the vase, which had been left on the floor under a tablecloth. She said—" Cairn paused, and chuckled. "She said it felt like the thing bit her."

"Serves her right for stomping around," I said lightly. I looked again at the little horse. This one was black, maybe onyx, with the same gold pole the others had; but in addition, it had an artful painting of a phoenix inscribed on each of its sides as it leapt through the air.

"I know when we were talking about them last night that you didn't think we'd be finding one so soon," Cairn said. Her smile had become almost maternal, as though *I* was the one whose shop had been broken into. "I wanted to tell you earlier, but Thorn said to be careful in talking about it. I thought . . . it'd be safest with you."

"Yeah, William has wards set up on our shop and everything." I leaned forward to pick the thing up, and could have sworn it shocked me through my glove.

"Maybe you can find something out about it," she suggested.

"I'll try. And in the meantime—you be careful, Cairn, just in case whoever did this comes back."

* * *

"Whoever did that," said William, after I'd brought him up to speed on the crime at Cairn's, "knows more than we do."

"Yeah, but not enough to make sure they broke through all of the vase," I pointed out. I'd settled in behind my workbench, goggles pulled down over my eyes, so I could study our newest acquisition.

William snorted. He was sprawled on the tile floor behind me; it wasn't all that hot in the backroom, particularly at twilight, at least not to me—but to a big fluffy dog, everything is hot. Apparently that holds true for dog-shaped familiars.

"Maybe the robbers were also idiots. Or maybe whoever knows about all this mess wasn't one of the robbers," he said.

I continued poking at the little horse with a quartz-tipped pick. "What do you mean?"

"Maybe someone was hired to do it." I didn't have to look back to know that William was rolling his eyes at me as he said it.

"Well, it's hard to say *what* happened. I didn't see much there to go on, aside from the mess. Unless the robbers really are idiots, and try to sell something from Cairn's shop nearby. Thorn's got her eye out, apparently."

"Maybe she ought to have that witch Trent make a spell to find the stuff. Or at least some better protection for the local shops," William said. "Not everyone can be expected to come up with the state-of-the-art protection I provide on their own. Maybe Ryuko was on to something—it's too bad you *can't* get the objects in the shop to talk."

"Animation of objects is a complex and *very* difficult endeavor, not to mention usually considered taboo," I reminded William. Generally he knew more about magic than I did, but alchemists often run into—or are mistaken for—tinkerers, and I'd had to leave more than one town because someone's 'animated intelligent home assistant' plan had gone awry. "And Trent was there earlier, but he can't trace anything that we don't have a trace of to begin with. I wish we could—I just—I just want to know where the other horse, if there was one, went."

I lapsed into thought. All I'd determined so far was that the paints on the black horse were a kind of ancient lacquer, the hooves were made of iron, and the horse itself was indeed onyx. It spoke in smooth, sepulchral tones which matched that dark rock exactly.

"The gold horse went into the pocket of one too blinded by greed to know its power."

Wait, what? I thought. For a moment I was no longer sure which sounds were aloud, and which were in my head. "William, did you hear—"

William was already on his feet and at my elbow, his fur tinged with the blue light that indicated he was channeling magic. "What have you done this time, Red?" he asked as he stared down the unmoving statuette.

"I didn't do anything," I protested. "I just said I wanted to know where the other horse went."

"And I have told you all I know on that subject," said the same oracular voice.

"Ohhhh dear." I pushed my goggles up on my forehead and squinted at the little horse. "You can talk?"

William and I both waited with bated breath, our heads pressing together as I bent down intently. I'm not sure what I was expecting. I could hear the voice just fine when my head was at a normal height. Maybe part of me was waiting to see if the horse's tiny mouth would move.

But it didn't.

William huffed. "I want," he said aloud, "for you to explain yourself."

"*There*," said the voice, "is something I have not been asked." Was it just me, or did it sound a little amused? "I am a Horse of Power, one who knows of firebirds and deepest seas and the Princess Vasilissa. How I came to be, I can not tell you. I have always been. I am here to serve and to help those who will listen."

I leaned my head in one hand, my fingers tangling through my long hair. "Well, the 'firebird' thing explains the art, anyway."

William was not to be distracted. "I want to know why you and your buddy were in that vase."

"I can not explain 'why' to you. I can merely assist you with *what* and *how*."

"What a weird charm." William shook his head and tried again. "I want to know how to find the gold horse, then."

"To find the gold horse, you must first find a person blinded by greed. They will be nervous, and you must reassure them. They will," the dark horse added compellingly, "be quite tall, with quick hands and heavy clothes, and smell like sweet incense."

William sneezed. "That was surprisingly helpful. Although, wouldn't everyone be tall to something only six inches high?"

"Oh dear," I said again. The specificity of the horse's account was unsettling, not least because I realized at once who it might be talking about. No one in town sold sweet incense—except the curiosities shop beside Cairn's. And someone who worked there happened to know all about the carousel horses. "Ryuko."

* * *

William and I set out as fast as we could. We left the iron-hooved horse at home, secured behind William's wards. William thought we might want it along for guidance but, as I pointed out, if we went in search of one horse and lost two, we'd need a lot more than guidance to get back on track.

Priya's shop was dark and jumbled full of things that smelled and things that moved. Priya was out when we got there, which was probably for the best: she and I weren't exactly friendly, even when I *wasn't* considering accusing her assistant of theft.

And it's not like I can outright accuse him, anyway, I reminded myself. *What did the horse say? 'You must reassure them.'*

We found Ryuko finishing his evening tidying-up.

"Oh, it's you," he began by saying. Not an unreasonable conclusion, but his indifference as he turned back to his mopping irked me, and my attempt at 'reassuring' fell flat.

"Listen, we wouldn't be here except for something important. I know you're busy and all, but could you tell us about anything odd that happened last night when Cairn's shop was robbed? Or maybe this morning?"

Ryuko squinted at me. "It's not like I live here, you know. Thorn already asked me a bunch of questions, anyway. This mean you're officially on the force?"

"I'm not with the police. I *happen* to run a shop—"

"They found evidence of incense from this shop in Cairn's," William interrupted. Surprised and fascinated by this sudden, bald-faced lie, I watched him with my mouth agape as he continued, "so, that means either your store got hit too, or someone who works here was there last night. Care to comment on that?"

I just want to point out that I am not the person who taught William to lie. But I'll admit I'm not above taking advantage of his mendacity. "It'd be better to talk to us now than to talk to Thorn later," I added hastily as William stared Ryuko down.

Ryuko heaved a sigh. "Think you're forgetting something."

"Facts don't forget," William growled.

"How 'bout the fact that I was at your apartment when it happened?"

"It actually happened after the meeting. But we're not accusing you, we're just curious," I said, backpedaling a little. The dark horse had said that the person we'd be looking for was nervous, but Ryuko was as unruffled as ever.

"I get it," Ryuko said, setting his mop aside, "but you're still forgetting—"

"What?" William interrupted again. "Are you going to tell us this place was broken into, too? It would explain the mess."

"Really, William, can't you at least *try* to be nice?" I hissed.

"You're forgetting," Ryuko practically shouted over William's retort, "that I'm not the only person who works here. Priya doesn't like Cairn. And she's been out on some 'communing with the forest' trip this whole time. Which, might I add, would be the perfect cover for coming back and committing some crime."

"Oh." I looked up apologetically. "You wouldn't happen to have any idea on how to get in touch with her, would you?"

"No." Ryuko eyed me for a moment, then shrugged. "Figures when I try to find a solid place for honest work, the boss goes and gets mixed up in crime."

"Yes, your self-pity is very interesting," said William dryly. "Do you at least know where Priya *lives?*"

Ryuko scratched absently at the back of his neck. "Well," he said at last, "We do get a lot of mail here at the shop that's been redirected from 012 Park Lane."

* * *

On our way to Park Lane, William and I had picked up Officer Thorn. And while normally I tried to avoid being within shouting distance of Thorn and William at the same time, in this case, it worked out for the best. Because 012 Park Lane wasn't empty and just waiting to be snooped around. Instead, as we climbed the steps to the ramshackle cottage's porch, the door swung open.

"What are you doing here?"

Not only was the speaker *home,* which I had doubted Priya would be (she had to keep up her cover, after all), it wasn't Priya at all. Priya was a knowledgeable if untidy human, rather small in stature. The person who greeted us now was a very tall, very anxious elf.

It was Priya's longtime shop assistant, Beth.

"Hey, Beth," I said, going for a friendly tone. William was already ruffled and Officer Thorn had her hand on her club, so it looked like it was up to me to broker peace. "Did anyone tell you what happened at Cairn's shop?"

I thought I did pretty well at light and neighborly. But Beth was having none of it. She pulled the door closed until only her pale nose and glittering eyes could be seen. "I don't know anything about it."

"Oh, you haven't heard? Ryuko did say you'd been out lately. Well—"

"I know about it already. I just don't *know* anything," Beth insisted.

William snorted.

I stepped closer, trying to think of what else to say. The porch beneath me creaked.

"I was just about to leave," Beth continued. "You should go."

Now *there* was something I could believe. By the looks of it, if we'd had to spend just one more second convincing the good officer to come along with us then we'd have missed Beth entirely. As I glanced into her living room through the crack in the door, I could see that her place was a mess. Her suitcase perched on an overflowing couch like even *it* didn't want to be there.

Seeing that, I figured that all the signs of guilt were present: nerves, standoffishness, a desire to flee. *Might as well go for it,* I thought. "Beth," I said, "we know all about it. We know why you want to leave."

"You know?" The revelation seemed to literally shake her,

from the tips of her pointy elf ears down to her slippered toes. "But you *can't* know!"

"We do," I insisted, trying to sound firm but friendly. "We heard all about it from—a very reliable source."

"Someone told you about my grandfather's fortune and the lost carousel horse?"

Bingo. Why yes, someone just did, I thought, trying to hide the triumph in my eyes. "Uh, yes. Now, everything can be okay. We just need you to turn in the carousel horse and anything else you might have taken."

In the shadow behind the door, Beth's face crumpled. "I only took what should have been *mine*." Her voice was now whining and strained.

"Right. I understand. But we're going to need it back." *Firm but friendly, firm but friendly . . .* "You do still have it, right, Beth?"

In the still, incense-laden air, Beth's teeth rattled. "I . . ."

"You what, Beth?"

"They said I—they said I had to send it on immediately, to be verified and insured—"

I stiffened. "Who said that?"

"Grandfather's lawy— wait. Didn't you say you know them?" Beth's gaze sharpened.

"What I know right now is that we're your friends, Beth. We're going to help you figure this out. We just need—"

"For sky's sake!" snapped William. "Enough!"

Like an arrow shot from a clumsy bow, William jumped headlong toward Beth. This meant bursting the door wide open, knocking Beth into her couch, and sending everything flying. Jars rolled, the suitcase tumbled. Officer Thorn dove into the mess, too. As William rose from the ancient cushions, a fine layer of dust coating his black fur, Officer Thorn popped back up holding Beth by the elbow.

"Good work," the officer grinned to the arcane familiar.

"Should've done that forever ago," William muttered, shaking himself loose of the ruins of the couch.

Beth pressed her hands to her face and began to cry.

"What's that for?" William regarded her like a small child might regard a monkey at the menagerie who's just stood up to deliver a lesson.

"Probably for all the furniture you just broke," I pointed out, as I followed my over-eager friends into the house. I waved a hand at the upended couch and the side tables rattled onto their sides.

"This wasn't supposed to happen!" wailed Beth. "It was just a simple job. Just a simple job! Get the horse and send it on! No one was supposed to know!"

William rolled his eyes at me in a look that said, *Sure, no one was supposed to know, until suddenly Beth was ten times richer than she'd ever been before and living in a mansion on the coast.* I couldn't help but wonder what her "grandfather's lawyers" had told her the horse was worth.

Still, it was nice of her to confess.

Officer Thorn cleared her throat and gave Beth a little shake—not unkindly; almost as if to remind her that she had an audience, and that audience had no idea what to do about her troubles. "There," she said to William, "is your answer, I reckon."

"Great. A fortune hunter seeking former glory, which was probably a lie to begin with." William sat, using one paw to shake the last of the dirt from his ear. "And we're too late for the horse, it sounds like. Well? Why stay here any longer?"

* * *

Naturally, we helped Thorn take Beth in and attempt to make sense of Beth's statement, not to mention find out who the "lawyers" were and what their address was. That they were actual lawyers I never believed for a moment. And when Beth confessed that she'd "discovered" the story about her grandfather owning a golden carousel horse in a packet of letters that showed up on her doorstep, I was ready to call the entire investigation quits. As I saw it, whoever had persuaded Beth to steal a tiny horse from a neighboring shop had been clever enough to cover their tracks.

By the time I got home late that night, though, I didn't feel like sleeping—not right away; instead, I sat at my kitchen table with a mug of chamomile tea. As I sipped, I thought.

I'd pulled out the horse from Cairn's shop once more, but I wasn't sure I felt like talking to it. Somehow, talking to the thing had only created more mystery. It had helped, sure, but we still lost the other statuette.

Minutes ticked by as I considered this, and all the mess and the confusion and the Council of War and the mysterious "them." Even if I were to ask the "Horse of Power" these things, it had said it couldn't talk about "why." And it only responded to questions prefaced with "I want." What did I really want to do?

Finally, very softly, I said to the horse, "I want to know how many little carousel horses there are. And I want to know what's so important about having them."

No spark brightened the dark horse's eye, and the phoenix in flight along its side never moved. But the graveyard voice said, "The horses come in ones and twos, and will be of great use to you. Collect the nine, and as they ride, they'll sing you the truth the world hides."

"Rhymes, great. Thanks." I sighed. *Another mystery. And, if nine is indeed the right number, that means six more horses to find.*

"Do not despair," the horse told me. I startled—I hadn't expected it to continue talking. "The trouble is not yet. The trouble is to come."

"Well that's . . . comforting." I frowned, but all the same I could see the sense in the horse's words. And, I resolved, if we were going to do it then we'd do it right. I vowed right then and there that next time I would not be late. I'd be there, ready to act, Council of War and plenty of guidance on my side.

And lots of cookies, too.

4

A Gold Shadow

The Fourth Carousel Caper

Sometimes I'd give anything to know *why* people do what they do. For example, why come into my potions shop in the middle of a busy festival and think that I have time for custom orders that usually take months to prepare? Why take one look at my magical canine companion and immediately start talking in baby talk? Why bother asking me to take coupons issued by the antiquities shop across the square?

And why anyone, even a ghostly do-gooder, would think that I'd have time to even *consider* leaving my shop during the afternoon rush was beyond me.

"But Rrred," Jade insisted. "Jade" is the nickname I'd given to an invisible and very persistent spirit of some kind. I've never been able to ascertain anything about Jade, except green eyes and a penchant for rolled *R*s. But after months of being in

Belville and dealing with Jade off and on, I'd started to develop a sense for when I was being followed. As I wove through customers and shelves, restocking potions and alchemical conveniences while William the wonder-dog manned the till, I had the feeling Jade was floating right at my elbow and talking directly into my ear. "The poorrr man is dead."

I paused. Normally I like my space, but I realized maybe it was a good thing Jade was so close that no one else could hear what was said in the bustle of the shop. "That sounds like a job for Officer Thorn, then," I hissed in no particular direction as I stuffed growth potions onto the nearest shelf.

"I'm sure she's there by now," Jade remarked with a suspicious amount of self-satisfaction. "But she'll need your help. I think it was poison."

"Oh you do, do you?" I sat back on my heels, wiping long dark hair out of my face. With a heavy sigh, I realized that Jade was right. The miracle was that Officer Thorn hadn't already beat down my door demanding my presence as her unofficial assistant. "And what exactly do *you* have to do with all this, Jade?"

"I was simply doing my rounds, and I noticed him lying beside the rroad outside of town."

"Rounds of what?" I asked absently, running calculations. How many more healing potions did I need? Could I potentially put off crime-solving until after I closed the shop for the day? "The pixies' Meeting festival? You don't strike me as a fair-goer."

"I always do rounds. I have to, if I want to stay frree."

"Mmhm. What?" snapped from my reverie, I looked up, but any trace of Jade was gone. Silently I cursed as I made my way to my backroom for more supplies, adding *what in Beyond does* that *mean?* to my list of unanswered questions.

* * *

Officer Thorn, half-orc, half-human, all business-and-puns guardian of the small town of Belville, did indeed show up soon after Jade had left. But I had been warned, and so was prepared: I asked her enough questions to keep her busy for an afternoon, and promised to go see her after she'd found some answers and I'd closed my shop. The last thing I wanted was to leave William, short-tempered at the best of times, alone with a slew of fair-happy customers.

"I looked for any of the traces you asked for, but there's no sign it was a crash," Thorn reported when I showed up at the police station as promised. "Some footprints in the mud, heavy, like maybe someone was carrying wares to the Meeting—doubt it was Kit, here, the victim, I mean. You knew him, right? One of the local mail carriers. Used to joke with everyone, you know, his nickname being 'Kit' and so many people yelling at intruders on their lawns, plus with him being catkin—"

"I get it," I told her. Officer Thorn nodded appreciatively; somehow her faith that I knew everything never faded, and perhaps that was what unnerved me the most about her. She was more subdued than usual, slouching behind the broad, messy expanse of her desk. Her usually perfect black hair was tangled and pulled back from the green skin of her face. I wondered briefly if Jade had insisted I help with the investigation for Kit's sake or for Thorn's.

"*Catkin.*" William, who had insisted on tagging along,

sneezed at my side. "Cat people are frightening," he muttered.

"Says the arcane talking dog," I said. "Ignore him, Officer. Did you figure out the cause of death?"

"Sure did." Officer Thorn pushed a glass bottle over the table toward me. Making sure I had my lab gloves on, I picked up the bottle gingerly. It seemed to have half a sugar cookie inside.

"Poison," the officer said, before I could ask anything. "Exactly like I suspected."

William huffed over my shoulder, his breath fogging up the glass. "How do you know?"

"I know because I found it when I went back to the scene. He'd dropped it, you see."

That wasn't enough for William, however. "But how do you *know*—"

"Red's going to test it, that's how." Officer Thorn rubbed her hands together as she focused on me. "That'll keep your mind off carousel horses, at least, right?"

If only.

Two days prior, Officer Thorn, William, and I had collected a mysterious dark carousel horse statuette—with the dubious help of Ryuko, who together with a bookstore clerk and an antiquities dealer made up what William had dubbed my Council of War. We'd lost track of another statuette, though, one we knew simply as "the gold horse." Supposedly, we'd been called to collect those strange horses, each of which contained a unique magic. Some said that together they could destroy the world, but I still wasn't sure *how*.

One question at a time, I reminded myself, taking my leave of Officer Thorn before William could start a fight. I set up my lab to distill bits of probably-poisoned cookie overnight and did my best to shove *all* matters crime-related from my mind, focusing on the sugar fairy cake William and I had snagged from some of the Meeting vendors. They'd been generous with leftover pastries and shishkabobs too, which was a stroke of good luck. I've never been the type who can skip a meal without succumbing to the depths of hanger, and the last thing I wanted to do that night was cook.

* * *

In the morning I had an answer, if only to the simplest of my questions. The cookie contained oleandrin, a toxin from a *very* poisonous—and in Belville, unusual—plant.

"You know," said Officer Thorn, who had stopped by at breakfast time bearing her habitual croissants, "Ryuko mentioned the other day he knows someone who knows how to find things."

"Oh he does, does he?" I lifted an eyebrow as I watched Thorn across my sales counter. Snakekin Ryuko had a shifty air about him, and even though he'd been nothing but helpful so far, I couldn't help but wonder how he knew such a person.

The Officer shrugged. "Not a crime to know people, Red. Sometimes you're just as bad as that dog of yours."

Fortunately William was still asleep in the apartment above the shop and couldn't hear the slight. I sighed. "The whole horse thing has made me suspicious. Sorry. So, are you saying you want to ask Ryuko's friend to find us some oleander? Or—"

"Or to find the missing horse," she suggested.

But I had been struck by a different idea. "Please, one mystery at a time, okay? Why not ask Trent to do a tracing charm? It's unlikely anyone but the murderer has an oleander on them."

"You want to bring the Witch in?" Officer Thorn stroked her long chin thoughtfully. "Don't tracing spells need something to trace?"

"Yeah, but I have some leaves he can use. Don't give me that look! In small doses, they're important for calming potions. What kind of alchemist would I be if I didn't have all sorts of this kind of thing?"

"And that," said Thorn, downing her tea with a wide grin, "is why I have you working *for* the law rather than against it."

* * *

Trent's tracing spell involved burning up the oleander leaves I'd given him, a bit of chanting, and an unpleasant moment where he flicked ash at Thorn and me. But the upshot of our temporary discomfort was that we could see with clarity a faint purple trail rising from the burnt oleander and weaving through town towards any other remnants of the plant. Sometimes I'm reminded why every town traditionally has a local Witch. They can be handy—even when they are teenaged and really just want to get back to their bacon.

Officer Thorn and I set off at once, following the purple smoke like Dorothy and her companions on the yellow brick road. In fact, as we crossed through town and headed for the forest, Thorn started skipping. I looked at her askance.

"I've known a long time there must be a hideout back here," she said self-consciously, "but I've never been able to find it."

"Great. So you think we're headed into a den of thieves?

Why would they have cared about the mail carrier?"

"Maybe he saw something he shouldn't have. Might even have to do with the—"

"Don't say it," I warned her. As the forest grew darker and the purple trail grew stronger, my voice lowered. "Maybe now would be a good time to make an escape plan?"

"Oh, come on, Red," said Thorn. She was moving more stealthily now, an impressive feat for a half-orc, but I was alarmed to see her holding her staff as though ready to deal a sharp blow to someone's stomach. "We have the law on our side. It's them who ought to be afraid of *us*."

For a moment I couldn't protest, as the purple smoke took an abrupt turn into a thick wall of weeds. I followed Officer Thorn into the brambles and at once the forest around us went quiet, darker. We were in the shadow of a large cliff that had loomed out of the undergrowth. We edged around it carefully, the ground sloping away beneath our feet. Above the mess of leaves and flowers, I caught a glimpse of a clearing and a break in the face of the rock ahead.

"*Thorn!*" I hissed. "Are you sure you don't want to make this just a reconnaissance mission?"

"Who's to say we'd find it again?" she pointed out. "No time like the present, as I see it."

"But we have no idea what's in that cave!"

"I know what's not outside it," said the officer reasonably. "Sentries. Look, Red."

I did—and she was right. I crouched and peered through the stalks in front of us, taking care not to be visible. The clearing ahead was below us, down a sharp slope, nestled right up against the rock outcrop we'd circled. The mouth of the cave stood like a cottage door looking over a neat little yard—a cottage sure to be full of outlaws and swords, that is. The dirt was bare and covered in boot prints. Yet despite that feeling of habitation, there was no one around—not in front of the cave, and nowhere on the cliff above, as far as I could tell.

Meanwhile, the purple smoke went glimmering right into that dark abyss.

I stood back up and looked at Thorn, who was grinning. I sighed.

"You're serious about this?" I whispered. Because I already knew the answer, my hand went to the dagger in my boot.

"Maybe they're out having a nice walk," said Officer Thorn.

"*Maybe* they're inside waiting to ambush us," I countered.

"'Snot an ambush if we know to expect it," Thorn replied confidently. She reached into the pack slung over one shoulder and brought out a handful of fine vials, the glass winking at me in the dappled sunlight. I recognized Solidifying Slime and Flash Powder inside the little containers.

"You got those from my shop!" I realized, affronted. "Officer, I run a store that helps people, not an armory!"

"Bought 'em off your assistant," Officer Thorn grinned, insinuating that William was running a weapons market out my back door. I was *definitely* going to have a talk with him when we got back. "Even though he refused to give me a lawmaker's discount."

"Well, don't feel special. William wouldn't give his own grandma a discount," I muttered. "Okay, fine. Great. We're going to slime the bad guys into submission."

"You're going to," Officer Thorn corrected, thrusting the vials at me. "And only if they don't respond to questioning. I'll go in first. Cover me!"

And just like that, we were storming the cave. Officer Thorn thundered into the clearing. I followed more cautiously. I couldn't stop looking over my shoulder. I *hate* dark, enclosed spaces. And ambushes. And the two together most of all.

Still, there was never any chance I'd leave Officer Thorn on her own. She must have known that, because she strode into that cave like she'd carved the place out of the cliff herself. Orcs, even half-orcs, have very good vision in the dark; and so do the people of my tribe, particularly when it's augmented by a pair of alchemists' goggles. With my handmade lenses protecting my face and the damp stone wall at my back, I edged along in Thorn's wake.

The channel through the rock was narrow, and rough. It smelled more like mold than a nefarious poisoner's hangout (for the record, yes I do know what such a place would smell like, but only because I work with the same ingredients making good stuff). Just as I was beginning to think that we were prowling over-cautiously around some abandoned cave, the purple smoke dipped down into a side channel and blossomed into a fog.

Officer Thorn and I stood huddled at the edge of a wide, wide cavern. Our path had emerged onto a ledge, which curved along the wall and dipped down to meet the floor below us. The ceiling was lost in fog, but the edges of the room were marked by lanterns casting a gentle green light. Dark spaces in the wall indicated other passages, but we had no time to be curious about those. Illuminated by the lamps, surrounded by chests and side tables, a long wood table stood in the center of the room. Rough-hewn benches clustered around it, supporting a dozen tough types chowing down on what smelled like wild turkey—except that they'd all stopped chewing and were staring directly at us.

"Come to join us for lunch, have you?"

The speaker had a lovely, deep voice. She sat at the head of the table and as she watched us, her mouth twisted back at one corner, like we were no better than poorly-dressed unwashed walking corpses. Her sand-colored skin and wave-colored hair gave her away as a coastal elf—probably as far from home as I was in this mountainous forest.

"Business, actually," said Officer Thorn. She introduced herself shortly while I did my best to fade into the shadow and take stock of the crowd. The elf seemed like the leader; everyone else looked like they'd mug beachgoers rather than sing the tide's praises. Some were human, some goblin, but I saw no more elves. I wasn't sure exactly what that meant, but I doubted everyone had gathered simply for a picnic.

"What business could you possibly have with us, Officer? And can it not wait until our lunch is done?"

"The dead can't wait," said Thorn grimly.

The elf's eyes narrowed. "And neither can you. That seems suggestive, don't you think?"

Officer Thorn paused and, behind her back, made some waving gesture at me that I did not understand. Then she stepped forward along the ledge, saying, "Justice'll take you whether you've got crumbs on your coat or not. But for right now, all we have to do is chat. Go ahead and keep eating, and why don't you tell me everything you know about Kit the mail carrier?"

In the darkness beside the tunnel mouth, I shook my head. Officer Thorn *was* always well-turned out, but leave it to her to insult the cleanliness of a bunch of outlaws! And just what was she expecting me to do? Ransack the place for clues? I might not have been introduced to the room, but I'd definitely been noticed. It's not like I could start creeping around with free rein just because she was asking them for testimony. Besides, the place was littered with tunnels; how would I even know where to go?

Suddenly reminded of the tunnel at my back, I wondered if Thorn's gesture had something to do with guarding the rear. Had she heard something coming? I tried to remain as still as possible while flicking my gaze over my shoulder. My spine was beginning to itch. I couldn't hear anything over Officer Thorn as she continued to argue with the coastal elf.

None of the shadows behind me moved. Not even the purple smoke wavered.

"Rrred, you made it. I didn't see you leave town."

Jade's voice floated from somewhere above my shoulder, nearly making me jump out of my boots. I did not appreciate the surprise, nor the reproachful tone.

"*Jade!*" I hissed, trying not to draw attention from Thorn's repartee with the elf regarding catkin. "You knew we'd end up here, didn't you?"

"I'm not omniscient. But I'll admit I am eternally hopeful."

"Hopeful that Thorn and I will get ourselves killed?" I whispered furiously. It was no use trying to see Jade, so I continued scowling at the lunchers.

"Of course not. How could you say such a thing?"

"Why are you even here? Did you see what happened to Kit? Is that why you've been hanging around? If you saw the murder, why couldn't you just have gone to Officer Thorn and said—"

"The Officer will not hearr me."

"*Ex*cuse me?" My head snapped up. I probably looked crazy to those bandits who weren't watching their leader hash it out with Thorn, but what did that matter? If Thorn couldn't hear Jade and no one else seemed to either, then maybe I really *was* crazy. Unless Jade just meant that Thorn wouldn't listen to some wild story about bandits killing Kit, which sounded very reasonable of her . . .

"I also," said Jade mournfully, "can not pick up the object I wished to give you. They have one of the horses, Rrred, the gold horse. It is herrre, inside a crate."

What? Jade's in on the horse thing too? And since when does "giving" mean "reappropriating stolen goods"? I took a very deep breath, tuned Jade out, and spent a moment reciting all the names of the great Seers of the desert—just like my mother had insisted when I was small and upset about some injustice. As I exhaled my eyes snapped open and I understood what I would have to do.

"Tell me exactly which crate," I demanded through gritted teeth.

"The one at the top of the pile by the tunnel to the right."

"Okay, fine. I'll check it out, but you have to cover for me and Thorn."

"How can I do that, Rred?"

"I don't know, can't you do something ghostly over the table or make one of them choke on a turkey leg or something?"

"I am not a ghost," Jade protested, a little petulantly. "And my talents lie in peaceful arts."

"'Peaceful' like knowing way more than you ought to?" I whispered back as I dug through my pack for the bottles Thorn had given me. "I'm going as soon as I throw this. Help somehow, I don't care how, just make sure Thorn doesn't get jumped. Please."

And because I was done arguing with Jade, and done with

being in the creepy cave with the elf who looked at me and my friends like we were beetles, and done with bandits and cursed horses, I threw all four of the slime bottles. Actually I didn't throw them; I hurled them violently into the table and on top of the bandits, one after another in rapid succession.

Thorn's diplomacy was cut off as the cave erupted in oozing green grossness. Slime potions have never been my favorite; the texture is downright unnatural. But they do the trick, if I do say so myself. By the time I'd made it around the ledge and to the boxes stacked by the other tunnel, that green muck had hardened into a crystalline shell strong enough to glue every single one of the bandits to their seats.

But it wouldn't last forever. I had maybe five or ten minutes, depending on how good my potion-making game had been when I prepared those bottles. I had no idea when Thorn had convinced William to sell them to her, so it was no use guessing. I tore into the pile of crates and boxes as fast as I could.

Meanwhile on the other side of the room the coastal elf was shouting. "Skar!! Skaab!"

Well, *those* weren't the names of friendly chefs. I could feel the lumbering footsteps reverberating throughout the cave.

It's gotta be here, gotta be fast, I thought. The sack at the top of the pile spilled, creating a waterfall of little tubes in my hands. Blinking rapidly, I recognized that this pile was of packages to be mailed. *Oh. Duh.* It made sense that the package Kit had known too much about, the one that most likely had ended his life, had been one of those cursed carousel horses.

What didn't make sense was Thorn yelling at me across the cacophony of the cave. "We got a live one! Live one! A little help, when you get the time!"

What? The footsteps hadn't arrived yet, and the bandits should have been glued to their seats. I looked out over the sea of heads to see Thorn pinned in one corner of the room by the elf, but at first I didn't understand why; she was no taller than she'd been when she was sitting at the table.

Because she's still sitting, I realized. The elf was perched atop the most cleverly designed wheelchair I'd ever seen. From across the bluelit cave, I could see its central sphere spinning across the floor like a droplet of water, supporting the shell-carved chair effortlessly.

While I was still stuck in the thrall of inventor's envy, admiring the workmanship on my enemy's wheelchair, the footsteps finally arrived. Skar and Skaab were not the fastest of allies, apparently, but that's because they were rock trolls. They emerged from the other end of the cavern like they were living rock detaching from the wall. They moved heavily, stooped, inevitable; the fluorescent moss draped over their thickly set heads and bulbous shoulders clearly marked them as they lumbered across the room.

"You called, Lark?"

"How is your lunch?"

I blinked. Maybe they *were* chefs. That'd serve me right for making assumptions.

"Lunch has been interrupted by two very rude guests," the leader, Lark, called. Her voice reminded me that I had a job to do, and time was running out. I knocked the sack of scrolls out of my way and began rifling through boxes, all the while trying to keep an eye on the mayhem.

"*I* was just hoping to chat, and here you come at me with a net and spear!"

"Be quiet, Officer. Skar, Skaab, would you see to the other

one?"

There was a hatbox with, unsurprisingly, a hat in it. I threw it to the floor and most of the other small crates followed.

"Of course, Lark."

"We're on it!"

I flew to the floor after the crates. Jade had said the horse was in one on top. Where *was* that meddling un-ghost?

"The law has things to say about netting an officer!"

"I should think you'd be honored. This net was made by the wavekin sorcerers, from only the very finest sea horses' manes."

The rock trolls' footsteps, which had been bearing down upon me as I tore the lids off box after box, stopped.

Thorn and Lark stopped arguing.

I couldn't bear it any longer. I paused my search. With a creeping sense of dread, I looked up to see—

Look, I know this is going to sound ridiculous, but at first when I looked up my first thought was *jellyfish disco*. All of the lights in the cavern had gone dark, something I hadn't noticed at first because I could still see well enough. But the contrast of the shadows with the streaky, flashing light of fluorescent moss waving through the air had a stupefying effect. There was an almost rhythmic grunting as Skar and Skaab lurched and swiped at each other, trying to save each other from their suddenly-animated moss. From across the cavern, their movements had the tone of a frenetic dance. I swear as I watched I heard Jade's speculative voice floating along the rock: "Moving moss is peaceful." Skar and Skaab, their eyes wide with alarm, seemed to disagree.

I slid back into the pile of packages, blindly searching now. My hand caught the edge of something smooth and warm and at first I jerked my whole arm back—but then at once plunged back in and came up with none other than a small, polished carousel statue. *The gold horse.*

Flush with success, I rose. I charged back across the room, rifling through my pockets as I went. I passed struggling bandits and barged past Lark, who was indeed wielding a net and spear. Not pausing to be afraid, I grabbed Thorn by the elbow and flung the flash powder vials to the ground at our feet.

Lark and her trolls reeled—but so did Thorn. I had to drag her back to the entry tunnel before she finally started moving on her own, her heavy legs pounding behind me as she shouted, "You could have warned me!!"

"About the moss seance?" I panted. We were full-on sprinting now, faster than I'd ever run before, scraping our shoulders on the slippery rock walls as behind us Lark roared. "Or about the flashes?"

"—could have—gone blind!!"

"You're the one who brought them along!"

"—that crazy—elf would've caught me—"

"Run faster, would you? We're almost there!"

"Not everyone's—a desert gazelle!" Thorn's words came in heaves and gasps now, but we were almost free. I clutched one hand over the horse in a pouch at my belt.

I spilled into the sunlight at last with Thorn several steps behind me. For a moment I stood, dazed, while the much larger officer caught her breath. Then we heard the rumbling from inside the cave.

Thorn's green eyes met mine. "No time to stop now, Red," she declared.

For the first time, we were in complete agreement.

* * *

"So," William summarized later that evening when the three of us were safe in my tiny apartment, "while I was stuck fighting with the cash register and slogging through endless smalltalk with customers with only Dusty to help me, thinking that my efforts were taxing but at least they were for the greater good, you two were out thieving."

"'Greater good,' ha!" I was pretty sure that hadn't been William's primary concern in manning the shop. He and the ubiquitous gnome Dusty were great friends, and had probably had a grand time while I was away. But I didn't press the issue. I didn't want to appear *too* ungrateful as I buried my face in a bowl of curried veggies William had fetched from the tavern.

"It's not thieving if it's from thieves," said Thorn with a characteristically easy conscience. She reclined across two of the chairs set around the little kitchenette table as she, too, devoured take-out curry. After she'd dragged me to the police station to give a complete report, she'd insisted on escorting me and the gold horse home. Personally I didn't think she was as worried about safety as she was intent upon hearing William's expert analysis of the latest carousel statuette, but of course she would never admit to any such thing. "And that wasn't all. You can mark my words, we'll have one of those bandits in for Kit's death before tomorrow's out."

My ravenous chewing paused, and I wiped my hair back from my face to look at the officer across the table. "What?"

"Come on, Red," said William. He took up the remaining chair by my side, his long tail colliding with the wall when he waved it disdainfully. "The curio shop clerk we caught last time said she'd just sent out the gold horse, then a few days later the mail carrier is dead. Could it be any more obvious that he was sent out to deliver the horse to the woods, saw too much, and was poisoned just to tie off loose ends? What do you want, a sign or something?"

"I *figured* that," I protested, scrunching my nose at him. "But I didn't think any of those bandits were confessing any time soon, and it's not like we got evidence."

"Too bad you didn't grab the crate as well as the horse," Officer Thorn said wistfully. Before I could protest, she continued, "But don't beat yourself up about it, Red. This is how things go with a criminal ring like this. I'll show up tomorrow with Police Guild paperwork, Lark'll give me a story about how one of her underlings went and slipped Kit something without her knowing, and one of the lackeys will come along and confess. Easy."

"And totally not just at all!" I protested. "Are you really saying you'll be satisfied with that?"

"We'll pretend. For now." Officer Thorn set down her bowl and grinned. "We've got an eye on them now, and they know it. Maybe the lackey'll turn on them after a few days of thinking in jail, and we'll learn more. If not, we're still going to keep after them, and it'll be a lot easier now that we know what we're looking for."

This was starting to sound like chess. Not a game I enjoyed. And certainly not real life. But, I reminded myself, real life didn't always come with answers, and it certainly didn't come with winners—not in the long run. The only thing we could do was keep trying.

"You see?" Officer Thorn leaned back, her arms behind her head. Seeing from my face that I did, she went on, "So how about a look at the most recent doodad, then?"

"Technically it belongs to Cairn," I said rebelliously as I fished the horse from my pocket. "It and the dark horse were stolen from *her* shop."

"And she told *you* to take care of them," William pointed out. He was already leaning across the table, his nose twitching as his gaze fixed on the frolicking horse.

I set it in the center of the table, carefully removing the potted herb—one of many—that served as a centerpiece. The plant rustled, filling my nose with the scent of lavender, helping me calm down. I knew what Thorn and William were waiting for, and as much as I was inclined to be stubborn, they were right. "Before you ask, yes, I took a look at it in the lab before dinner. As you can see, it's not actually gold—just the mane and tail and the pole are. The body is a polished cloudy quartz. Oh, the saddle and bridle details are gilded too, but aside from that—"

"You sure?" Officer Thorn interrupted. "What if it's white gold?"

I glared at her. "I think I'd know the difference, Officer. White gold is harder than normal gold, sure, but still not—"

"Maybe they just *thought* it's all gold," she interrupted again.

"Will you two stop bickering?" William sneezed, rocking the table and sending the horse sliding. "The whole 'gold horse' thing was obviously metaphorical. It's not *made* of gold, it's *worth* gold."

He looked up at me expectantly, and I held up my hands. "Listen, you're the one with the arcane knowledge about why it might be worth something or how it's been charmed. I'm just here to talk about science. White quartz *has* traditionally been associated with wisdom, I guess, but that's all I got."

"Why would a group of bandits be after the thing?" Thorn had leaned back and was muttering. "That Lark didn't look like she was running a fool's operation. If they want money that's one thing, but if it's something else then what is it?"

William cocked his head, his dark eyes moving between the horse and me. "When you came home you had traces of it on you," he told me. "At the time I figured it was remnants of the Witch's tracing spell, but it wasn't. The aura on you matched the spell on the horse. What did it do?"

"I had a spell on me?" I ran my fingers through my hair. I believed William as a matter of course: as I'd reminded him, he was an expert in arcane matters, and—being magical himself—could often sense magic in a way other people could not. "Thorn, did you notice anything?"

"I had my hands full just trying to keep up," she remarked. "The only times I felt like you weren't about to bolt out of sight was when you were pulling me along. How could I have noticed anything?"

"You *did* notice something," said William, his tail thunking against the wall. "That was the spell. Speed. That horse—the quartz reminds me of ice, so I was thinking Norse already, but I wasn't sure. It's Gullfaxi, or maybe an artistic Sleipnir. The fastest horses the Norse gods knew."

"Huh." I sighed. "At least it doesn't talk like the dark horse did."

"That still doesn't explain why it was worth gold. And a man's life!" Thorn protested. But the day had been a long one, and William and I were quite happy to leave the conversation at that.

* * *

And so my collection of charmed carousel horses had grown to four. I found myself thinking about them as I closed up shop the next day. A drowning spell, a storm spell, a speed spell, and an enigmatic "I'll tell you how to get things" spell. Since the dark horse had told us about the "gold" horse, I guess I'd assumed that the gold horse would talk too. In a way, it was almost too bad it wasn't some kind of spell to tell me not how but *why*.

"Some mysteries are bound to be," I murmured to my reflection in the polished sales counter as I finished dusting.

"Hello, Rrred," said Jade cheerfully.

"Mother Earth and heaven above us!" I swore, twisting around—not that it did me any good, because I only caught a glimpse of green eyes. "Jade, could you *please* stop doing that? Ring the bell or something when you come in!"

"I was going to," Jade insisted. "Do you think I would spy on you?"

"Well you seem just fine spying on everyone else," I said, scrubbing at the already-clean counter.

"Only the murrrderrous ones."

I let the point lie, not wanting to argue. But I couldn't stop thinking about Lark and her cavern and her lackeys, and the little horse in the crate. "Why didn't you tell me at the beginning that this whole thing was because of a carousel horse?"

"You wouldn't have gone," said Jade. "Would you?"

"I . . . Probably I would have. It's not like I have much choice. These things find me."

"*You* found *it*," Jade reminded me deliberately. "You play the reluctant hero well."

My hands slowed over the counter and my breath went still,

the lemony cleaning potion smell stuck in my throat. "What's that supposed to mean?"

"That we are alike, you and I. And because you are here, justice will be done." Jade paused, and added quietly, "I am grateful for that."

"Well, don't get ahead of yourself." I leaned against the register, blowing hair out of my face and thinking about the encounter in the cave. "I ought to be thanking you for—whatever you did yesterday. Even with the spell on the horse, I don't think the Officer and I would have made it out otherwise. So tell me . . . why *couldn't* you pick it up? And why were you keeping tabs on it in the first place?"

"The gold horse, you mean." Jade spoke very slowly. "The purpose of carrousels is to create a fantasy. These statues are a danger to reality."

"Uh huh. And how do you know that?"

"Call it . . . personal experience."

The light of the setting sun swept across the shop, winking off potion bottles and polished wood. The only sound was the rise and fall of my breath, and the chatter of happy passersby in the square outside.

I sighed. "Alright, Jade, I'll give you that one. That's why the horses are so valuable, isn't it. They're weapons, somehow?"

"Valuable to desperate people," said Jade, sadly. "You must be careful, Rred."

"Well, that's getting harder and harder the more criminal organizations I run across," I muttered. "And why it should be *me* in charge here is still another mystery unexplained."

But no one—not a false ghost nor a talking horse—had any answer. I decided I might as well resign myself to the mystery of it, at least for the moment.

In time, I'd find out all the answers to my questions, and more.

5

A White Wind

The Fifth Carousel Caper

High on the list of Impossible Things To Do is "find a quiet place to think when you live in a small town that's currently hosting a bunch of sorcerers and pixies for a magical festival." Seriously, every time I settled into a thought—usually about the charmed and dangerous carousel horse statuettes that had taken over my life—someone rustled me out of it by starting up a folk tune, lighting off a firecracker, or ringing my shop bell after hours. I'd given up on thinking at all while in Belville. Instead, I'd fled to the forest outside of town, telling my assistant William that I needed to gather more herbs for my alchemy. What I really wanted to do was disappear, just for a little while.

Though I grew up on a desert island, I'd become perfectly at home in the forest. The abundance of plants and minerals was one of the reasons I'd chosen Belville as the place to open my dream alchemy shop. Here, I could get a lot of my ingredients for free—provided I had the time to gather them, and the concentration to tell Hallowing Root from Harrowing Stalk or shiny green copper ore from druidic boundary markers.

I was following one such vein, my knees on the mossy ground and my alchemists' goggles pulled over my eyes, breathing in the smell of dirt and not much caring about whether I would run into druids or not, thinking to myself *no one could possibly find me now*, when bushes rustled behind me and someone let out an "*aha!*" of triumph.

"See, I told you this felt like the right place," the triumphant voice continued. I didn't recognize the speaker, but the accent was familiar. *What in the wide, wide world?* Wondering why a stranger from my homeland had come all the way to pastoral Belville, I begrudgingly rose to my feet.

"Good thing, 'cause the woods up to the left are s'posed to be haunted, you know. Not that it matters."

As I turned, I saw not one but two interlopers. I was familiar with Ryuko, a tall and often sullen shop clerk with the dark skin and scales of the snakekin, a race of people with snake-like attributes. That he was too cool to be worried about haunted forests, I did not find surprising. What surprised me was the girl with him. Short, nut-brown, dressed in layers of bright purple and wearing her cropped hair in braids, she was definitely from one of the desert tribes.

"I'm Clarity," she announced, dropping her hold on a berry bush to offer her hand to me. The leaves from the released plant flew into my face as I dumbly extended my own hand. "You can call me Clare. Ryuko said you needed help finding magic statues, but I think *you* were harder to find than they are."

"That was kind of the idea," I mumbled. Dimly, I remembered hearing that Ryuko had asked a friend of his to help us in the search for the horses. *The further I try to get from this mess, the harder it tracks me down. Well, alright, nothing for it,* I decided. "I'm Red, as you probably already heard. Thanks for coming all this way to help us. So, you found a carousel horse too?"

"Oh it wasn't that far," Clare laughed. "I've been living in Brass, you know, the 'magitech capital of Beyond'? That's where Ryuko found me. And as for the horse—"

"Tell stories later," Ryuko interrupted, shimmering in the shadow of the trees. "It's s'posed to rain. Come on."

"You're just afraid of the ghosts," teased Clare as she fell into step behind Ryuko as he led us back toward town. Despite my misgivings, I went too, musing. I've never been the best at guessing kids' ages, but Clare seemed fourteen at most. And for as carefree as she acted, I noticed as we walked that she was hanging on to Ryuko's long coat.

"*Red* would never be afraid of ghosts," Clare added over her shoulder, shaking me out of my thoughts. "Right? My uncle told me the members of your tribe never are."

"Ahhh, no, nope, not afraid," I stuttered, sounding like a lying fool, not because I cared about hauntings but because I had never told anyone in Belville about my tribe. Still, I reminded myself, it wouldn't have been hard for Clare to guess. There are four tribes in the islands of the Sifting Sands, each with their specialities and customs. To the outside eye they all seemed basically the same, all Seers, but where one tribe focused on fate, another focused on love, and so on.

Speaking of which, Clare was still looking back at me, grinning, and her dark eyes seemed to see right through me. When the sun peeked out suddenly from the clouds, flashing across her face but not prompting any change in her expression, I finally realized that Clare was blind.

"You're probably wondering which one I'm from," she continued merrily as we splashed across a small stream. "My people are the Followers of the Sphinx. But I've never been able to do prophecy or riddles. Instead, I was born able to see where missing things are. That's how we found you just now."

Thanks for that, I could have said. *Couldn't you simply have waited at my shop?* But honestly the last thing I needed was for William to have a chance to grill a real seer about my absolute lack of Seer-ness. And besides, Clare was so cheery it was hard to be resentful. I said, "Is that how you found a carousel horse? But they aren't technically missing. They're more often hidden. Does that still work?"

"It worked for one of them," Clare told me confidently. "And it's a whole lot closer than you think."

* * *

Ryuko, Clare, and I got back to my shop, Red's Alchemy and Potions, at lunchtime—that is to say, just as William was waking up. An arcane familiar who had long ago lost his sorcerer and now instead hung out around me, William was a big furry dog-shaped ball of wit and grumpiness. And, apparently, *not* reliability when having promised to open someone's store.

"There's a sign," William yawned. "Didn't you see it on the front door? We're closed until one o'clock. After all the business we've done during the festival, we deserve it."

"That isn't how business works," I protested, but chose not to pursue the fight. Instead I introduced Clare. Ryuko and I faded back between the potion shelves as she told William all about her skills—and her vision.

"Wait," said William just before she was done. "You're saying Ryuko asked you to conjure up a vision about a light horse, and you think you found one lost in a bag in the forest, and now you want us to go out there when it's full of spirits and cavorting sorcerers to look for the thing?"

"A white horse," Clare nodded, clarifying. "It's not exactly what Ryuko asked but it's definitely a carousel horse, and you guys need all of them, right?"

"Why'd you ask for a white one in the first place?" I asked Ryuko as we stood on the edges of the conversation.

He shrugged. "I couldn't remember what color Thorn said it was, only that the other one they found was dark. I figured, light and dark, right? But when I said 'light' the distance-speaking spell was wearing thin."

"Light and dark," I echoed thoughtfully, turning back to watch Clare deal with William.

"We'll be fine," she was telling him. "I know it's somewhere nearby—I'll be able to feel when it gets close."

"So we wander in the woods and hope that none of the ghosts who've moved in are the souls of recently-departed eager for us to join them." William sneezed, his shaggy black ears flopping.

I decided it was time for me to intervene. "Come on, William. It's not like anyone's actually been murdered in the woods. All that ghost talk is just, well, festival talk, that's all. And if Clare's right and the horse is lost, then we might not even have to deal with anyone at all—just find it and get back here."

"Uh huh. And of course, you're going to want to do this at

night," William observed, his beady eyes watching us like we were unruly children.

"Well, you have a shop to run during the day, right?" asked Clare sweetly.

"I actually have to work for Priya tonight. It's the only time Dusty can be there to help us with the safes. Been doing inventory since Beth ended up going," Ryuko added to me as an explanation. "Going" was apparently snakekin for "attempting to steal a dark carousel horse and succeeding in stealing a gold one, then ending up in jail." I nodded. He added to Clare, "You'll be alright?"

"I'll be fine with Red and William," Clare beamed. "Don't worry, Ry. We know exactly what we're doing!"

* * *

We had no idea what we were doing.

Clare, William, and I had been scouring the forest outside of town since I'd closed up shop for the day. Clare had barely allowed me time to grab a bagful of dinner before hustling us out onto the hillside. At first I had naively hoped this was because she could "feel" exactly where to go and was eager to lead us right to the place—but hours of roaming the woods essentially playing "hot and cold" had shown me the error of my assumptions.

"This is good," Clare informed us encouragingly. "I am definitely feeling it more strongly now."

"Great," William snorted as he leapt over a fallen tree. "Because we're headed straight to the haunted part of the forest."

I was at the front, having taken over Ryuko's responsibility of making sure Clare didn't run into any trees while she was focused on how near or far our missing carousel horse might be. The farther we went along the hillside, the less underbrush there was. The tree trunks rose up thick around us, casting deep shadows. A breeze overhead shook the branches and filled the forest with a restless sound. My eyesight was good in the dark, but all I could see was the occasional bat. All I could smell was damp bark.

"You're not worried about being haunted, are you?" Clare was asking William behind me. "You smell like magic."

"I *am* magic," William retorted. Without looking back I knew exactly what he was doing: tossing his floppy ears proudly. "Of course I'm not worried. But it'll be a nuisance trying to find a magic statue with shades of the damned or whatever mumbling in your ear."

"Is that what's here?" asked Clare as though we were discussing a new kind of bird or an unusual cache of fossils. "Red, what kind of haunting is it?"

"Just the average dark and spooky stuff. Nothing to worry ab—" My word was choked off as something big and black dropped from the sky. I swear it was headed straight from the treetops to my face. I ducked at once, and it *whoosh*ed harmlessly over all three of us.

I glanced back: Clare was unfazed, William was sniffing the air. He shook himself and turned to me with the doggy equivalent of a wry look. "What was that, Red, scared of a little wind? Easier not to worry about it when it's not aimed at you, huh?"

"Shut up," I retorted, not without affection. After all, he had a point. Despite what I'd told Clare, my skin was covered in goosebumps. "It wasn't just wind."

"I felt it too," Clare said. "Something cold. Are there more?"

"Probably," said William as we began walking again—this time more slowly. "There's got to be a whole pack of them, given the rate at which people've been seeing 'em. Who knows, given her directional abilities, Red might end up leading us right into their lair where they eat children and perform dark rituals to take people to the Other Side."

"William!" I remonstrated. Clare's hand had tightened on mine, but I realized that was because another frigid, shadowy shape was coming at us from the side. It darted out from between the trees and immediately disappeared, leaving my spine tingling.

"You're right, it's probably not rituals. Those would leave arcane traces which I, being of many talents and very sharp senses, would be able to see. Instead, I bet you all those eyes watching us from that weirdly-dark shadow over there are going to come together into one huge monster that's going to demand a blood sacrifice to create its own—"

"Really," I interrupted, swatting in his direction and looking to the right to see that there were, indeed, glowing eyes looking back at us. Most disconcerting was the fact that not all of them were paired. "What is wrong with you? Why do you always have to leap to the worst conclusion?"

"Maybe it just wants help," Clare agreed with me. I blinked and the eyes multiplied, spreading between the trees like a plague. It was now too dark to see where my feet were going, even with my darkvision, but I kept leading Clare forward.

"Look, no offense," said William, in what I recognized as one of his most offensive tones, "but that's just . . . meh. It's boring. Where's the rush, the defiance of taboo? *Everyone* needs help.

But you know what everyone doesn't do? Come at you with a storm of vines edged in blades and demand vengeance for—"

"Don't give them any ideas!" Clare was starting to sound distinctly nervous. When I looked back at her, I saw why.

A darkness too deep to see the forest or the stars loomed right behind Clare. The girl shrank in comparison. As I watched the darkness moved, a heavy footstep reverberating underneath my own thick boots. Red light, nothing like moonlight but perhaps like the gaze of all those eyes, glinted off what looked very much like a fang.

"Time," I said very softly. "To. *GO!*"

I yelled the last word, hoping it would startle the monster—and that for once William would actually listen. I tugged Clare into a sprint and hoped she could keep up, because once I start running it takes a force of nature to get me to stop.

Behind us the creature breathed so loudly it was like the forest itself was gasping for air. With each snap of a twig or rip of a vine, I could have sworn I heard small voices crying *get out!*. The night had gone absolutely glacial. As I puffed between the trees, my feet falling heavily and my arm pulled back, I felt like a troll trying to race through a clothesline.

I worried most about keeping Clare safe. The strange spine-tingling sensations of earlier had passed, and I was far from being scared witless. What Clare had guessed about me and my tribe was true. *Now,* I thought to myself as I ran, *I just have to get her to whatever place she saw in her vision and get her out. With our luck, what we want is probably exactly what all these spooks are trying to keep us away from.*

Maybe this, I realized wryly, *is the power of the "white horse" Clare found. The red one could call down storms; why not one that can conjure ghosts? I never did ask her if she knew what it could do*

. . .

"Can you hear me?" I panted to Clare as we continued to dodge tree trunks and specters like footballers going for the endzone. When she squeezed my hand, I continued, "Are we going the right way? Do you feel anything?"

"I—yeah, there's something!"

"Good." My foot slipped, and we both lurched sideways. "Which way?"

Her fingers tightened on mine "Let me think . . ."

"Think—fast!"

"I can't tell. I can't tell because it is so close! It's here!"

Surprise hit me and I stopped on a dime.

Clare collided with my spine as I looked around. We'd gone a ways up the hillside; it was a good thing Clare had said she'd found the thing, because we were right next to a dirt ledge that I might have run right into a second later. The trees around us were thinner, the eyes and footsteps were gone. Just a faint smell of ash and sulfur and the silent stars above us remained.

"Thanks," Clare said uncertainly, then promptly sat in a heap with her back against the ledge. "Sorry, I . . . I mean, wow. Everyone knows about Springers being fast, but that was *wild.*"

I chuckled at her reaction to my running. "You should have seen me a few days ago, with one of the carousel horses that has a speed charm. No ghost alive could've caught us then." Clare laughed, and I shrugged at the poorly-chosen word, grinning. "You know what I mean."

"Yeah."

After a moment's hesitation, I dropped down onto the ground beside her, thinking how strange it was that she *did* know exactly what I meant—and furthermore, that I didn't mind it. I'd been away from home—scratch that: I'd been *covering up* my home for so long that this kind of camaraderie had totally faded into memory. "Well, I didn't mean to scare you. But I guess you figured out from my name which tribe I was from?"

Clare couldn't read my expression, but I'm pretty sure she read my voice just as easily. "Ryuko had no idea, but I figured the only Seers with color names like yours are Springers. If you didn't want people to know, why didn't you change it?"

"It's . . ." *Complicated,* I wanted to say, but what came out was more honest. "It's silly, really."

"Ooooh, excellent," a strange voice floated down from above us. "I could use a little comedic relief!"

* * *

In short order, Clare and I found ourselves arranged around a lavish campfire. Somehow I wasn't surprised when William came panting up the ledge from a different direction. Any questions I had for him had to be set aside, because our host—a very thin, tall man with flowing (magical?) hair and robes for days, just in case we hadn't already figured out he was a sorcerer—talked nonstop from the moment he saw us leaning against the cliff.

"—and you *must* stay for dessert, I just set it out. I do *love* a good party. Ah, 'But Gilbert!' you ask. 'If you love a party, why are you going to the trouble to keep people away from your campsite with spells and sorcery? Why camp so far from the Meeting at all?' But you see the answer is very simple. I like a *smart* party. I can't bear inane chatter and wide-eyed curiosity and platitudes. In my opinion anyone who hasn't studied something shouldn't bother talking to me at all."

In the bright firelight, I raised an eyebrow at William. He was busy staring at the plethora of lush purple buildings surrounding the fire. For one lone camper, Gilbert the sorcerer seemed to have brought along a series of bungalows rather than a single tent. I suppose when you have magic to do the set up for you, why not go big?

"So you're the one behind the haunted forest?" Clare asked, ignoring the chocolate cake Gilbert pressed into her hands.

This finally caught William's attention. "It isn't haunted. It's *spelled*," he realized, flopping down to put one paw over his nose.

"Of course, you wouldn't have known that at the beginning, being merely a familiar," Gilbert told him—not unkindly. Offering another slice of cake to me, he continued, "Familiars can sense a great deal of magic, but the good sorcerer is a cut above such perception. And I had reason to make this spell as good as possible. Have you ever noticed how crowded and *noisy* Belville is?"

"Yes, I have," I answered dryly. "And we're sorry to have interrupted your solitude. You see, we're looking for—"

"No, no, not at all! To have got past the ghosts, you must be interesting enough for dessert, at least."

"But we're looking for something," Clare insisted, picking up the thread I'd left off. "And you might be too. Something that's lost. But it's right here, close by."

"Is it?" Gilbert sat down on what seemed through the smoke to be a gilded chair—no fallen logs or overturned stumps for seats here!—with his own piece of cake, and began casting his gaze from tent to tent. "Is it my tea cup from this morning? I left in a hurry, and forgot to take it with me. And then I never can seem to find my *nice* parchment, I used to keep it in this little carved case I found in an antiques—"

"It's a horse," I interrupted. I appreciated Clare's effort to be discreet, but somehow I doubted our concerns and Gilbert's concerns matched up anyway. "A little carousel horse statuette."

"White," Clare added helpfully. "With roses and a gold pole."

"Ah, the Wind Horse!" Gilbert looked at us fondly—at least I hoped it was fondly: unless the sparks from the fire lined up just right, it was hard to see the expression in his unnaturally dark eyes.

From the ground to my right, William groaned.

The sorcerer continued, "A very interesting piece, that. You see there are many societies who believe the Wind Horse has a connection to the human soul. One group in particular's got a very nice flag with the horse in the middle—you may have seen it. No? Well, I am a bit of a collector of these odd things, you know. So anyway I had found this one in a delightful little market near the Shifting Sands and thought—oh, but you're right! I haven't seen it in ages!"

I could see now why William, who was more accustomed to the ways of sorcerers, had groaned. Jaw clenched, I tried to get the conversation back on track. "Our friend here can find missing things, if you're okay with us moving around camp a bit. We'd be glad to pay you for it if we can find it, and then we'll be out of your hair."

"Oh, no!" said Gilbert, as though I'd suggested stealing his pants. "I don't need your money. Besides, I have no idea what I paid for it. Lost the receipt ages ago, you know. By all means find the thing, have it! And then I insist we have dessert like civilized people."

"Wait," said Clare. "Does the Wind Horse's power have to do with souls? Is that how you made the hauntings?"

"My dear child, I am perfectly capable of creating the appearance of a haunting on my own. Did you like how I put in all the normal haunting things? The whooshes, the shadows, the fangs? I could have gone more esoteric, of course. But then would the average townsperson have understood? You have to give the people what they know, you know. But now that you mention it . . . maybe it *was* the Wind Horse that gave me the idea. You see, the Wind Horse is a potent symbol of the fortune of the soul. Elemental, even, some have called it. The moment I picked up that statuette, I could feel the currents of energy all around me. How did you know?"

Clare shrugged in my direction, then set aside her cake carefully and rose. "Ryuko told me that's why they're important, that each horse has a power."

"Great. Water horse, storm horse, talking horse, speed horse, now we have elemental spirit horse," I sighed. My suspicions earlier had been right, it seemed. Maybe I was developing a sense for these carousel horses. "Come on, Clare, I'll help. William, are you just going to lie there?"

"Of course not!" Gilbert answered for him. "William and I are going to be good friends. He'll catch me up on all his adventures while you two go find that horse. Do tell me where it got to, won't you? I have a professional curiosity. Don't mind the socks . . ."

I took Clare's hand, tuning the sorcerer out. She giggled a little as we moved into the shadows beyond the campfire, but soon became all business: we were playing hot and cold once more. We bypassed the largest tent, poked our heads in another and quickly withdrew, then began sorting through a tent that seemed to serve mostly as a closet—not that there was anything like a hanger in sight. In an old linen bag behind the lining of an even older trunk, I finally found what Clare had seen. The Wind Horse.

It was lovely. Probably the first of the carousel horses I'd seen that I could actually picture being, well, an innocent carousel horse. The body was finely crafted glazed pottery, legs and mane curling gracefully. Being careful not to touch it directly, I tucked it into a pocket and we returned to the campfire.

"Found it, have you? Already? Where was it? Ah, that old trunk! It's probably hiding even more than we know. But it looks so nice with the whole ensemble, I can't bring myself to give it up. No, don't talk to me about money again, just take the horse and eat your cake.

"Obviously," Gilbert continued, beaming as we took our places and did as he said, "you have far more use for this horse than I. I had forgotten all about it. I've been very preoccupied, you see, with this new paper I've been writing on the intricacies and—between you and me—the fallacies of the High Order of Light Sorcerers, who—and I don't care who you tell this to—are just a bunch of hare-brained idiots. I say very clearly on page 87 that . . ."

* * *

And just like that, after trial by fake ghosts and chocolate cake, I had another carousel horse statuette to look after. As soon as we brought it home that night, I put it away in a specially-charmed safe that William had made. Cute as it was, I made sure that I only handled the horse while wearing gloves. I'd had my fill of ghosts or spirits or elemental luck, or whatever it was that Gilbert had said.

"So," I addressed William the next morning. We were both a bit bedraggled and bleary as we assembled over a very late brunch. "You didn't want to stay on as Gilbert's familiar, eh?"

"He certainly knows how to camp," William mumbled. There were still twigs caught in his fur from our late-night trip back into town. "But he wasn't *my* sorcerer. He's got a toad or a crawdad or something."

"Does he? I'm sure there's room for one more." I chuckled as William buried his head in a bowl of oatmeal, refusing to dignify my comment with a response. In the silence, I couldn't help but voice a question that had haunted my dreams. "Hey, if there are nine carousel horses altogether, and this spirit horse is the fifth one—you don't think they're all going to be, well, *spooky* from here on out, do you?"

William glanced up at me and licked oats from his nose. "This whole thing was pretty spooky to begin with, wasn't it? What with the horses showing up out of nowhere, and criminals trying to steal them."

"Sure," I agreed, "but that's a more practical kind of spooky. I can deal with that."

"And you can let me deal with the ghosts and magic," William reminded me, his fluffy tail wagging behind him. "That's our deal, right?"

"Right."

"Unless more wacky seers show up," William added. I chuckled again, knowing that he meant the term affectionately as he referred to Clare. *Maybe he's glad I don't do the 'Seer thing',* I realized. The thought eased a burden inside my soul that I hadn't known I'd been carrying. "Anyway, Red," William went on, "it's not actually a spooky horse, you know. It is what you make of it."

I wrinkled my nose at him. "Currents of spirit energy seem spooky to me."

"So would poisons like arsenic or mercury, but you use those to make good things in your experiments," William pointed out. "When Gilbert said that about energies, what he meant was the horse was guiding him. Sort of like giving him advice on where to go next."

"Oh. Well, that sounds helpful, actually. So why would he let something like that get lost?"

William shrugged. "Same reason you were so suspicious of it in the first place. Sorcerers may use flashy magic, but the good ones don't want to become dependent on it. 'When magic is in control, you *aren't*.' That's what Gilbert said while you and Clare were ransacking his camp."

"We weren't ransacking," I protested playfully. "But I'm glad you're around to translate sorcerer-speak."

Just as we were finishing up, the bell at the front door of the shop tinkled. I tossed my bowl in the sink and jogged down the stairs to find Clare on the porch with Ryuko looming over her shoulder, looking just as tired as the rest of us.

"Guess inventorying's a hard job," I said, looking him over.

"You didn't totally believe me," he replied, just as coolly, as Clare wandered into the shop. "But it isn't like that, Red. Sure, I wasn't always what Thorn would call 'legit,' but I'm really here trying to start over."

Officer Thorn was the local police, so technically, what she *wouldn't* call "legit" came with punishment attached. But I bit my tongue. It hadn't been my intention to judge Ryuko.

"I love the spices you use," Clare said from among the tables and shelves, all filled with potion bottles and ingredients. "It smells like home."

"Some are the same, I guess," I admitted as I followed her inside. Ryuko nodded to me and stayed on the porch to wait.

"I told him I just want to talk to you before I leave," Clare explained, her voice quieting. "I have to go back to Brass, but I'm glad everything worked out and that I was able to help. And—I wanted to tell you I didn't say anything to him, about you, and what we talked about in the forest. But I don't understand why you'd want to keep it a secret, Red."

"It's not a secret exactly." I hesitated, thinking of what Ryuko had said the day before about light and dark. Opposites—that's how I had come to think of the two halves of my life. Being an alchemist and being a seer don't mix: they're two totally different ways of looking for the truth. And yet at the same time, as he had pointed out, opposites did have a tendency to go together . . . and maybe Ryuko wasn't the only one who'd been trying to make a new start, only to be plagued by the past.

And maybe, like the mysterious Wind Horse, Clare's presence was guiding me to see something I hadn't noticed before.

"I get it," Clare said when I'd been silent too long. "Uncle always said that's why Springers are the most rare. It's because of all the pressure, right? Like instead of just focusing on a little part of seeing, like finding stuff or looking into the future, they're trying to see *everything*. The whole truth. Right?"

"Something like that," I agreed, though I wasn't entirely sure what I was agreeing to. Technically Clare was right: that was the focus of my tribe. Truth. I hadn't ever thought of it as *pressure* before, but maybe she was onto something.

"Don't you think that's why you're doing this, though?" Clare's short braids shook as she tilted her head. "Don't you think that's what solving all these mysteries is about?"

"I . . . who knows," I sighed. But I smiled as Clare came in for a hug, and bid her farewell.

"Good luck with the rest of them," she whispered on her way out.

I had a feeling, particularly after everything she'd given me to think about, that I was going to need all the luck I could get.

6

A Coal-Black Ride

The Sixth Carousel Caper

Having superpowers isn't all it's cracked up to be.

Or so I surmised as I looked at Luca. Ostensibly he was a simple bookstore clerk; but while the recent days had kept me busy running after magical carousel horses and associated murders, Luca—if the Belville rumor-mill was to be believed—had been busy stopping runaway carts, rescuing small children from certain death, and single-handedly preventing rock slides. In a little town hosting a big magic festival there's no end of need for the miraculous. Luca looked like he'd paid the toll: under his habitual black robes, his dark brown skin was sagging, and his green eyes were red-rimmed.

"I think this is the first time you've come to *my* shop, instead of the other way round," I observed, waving him further into Red's Alchemy and Potions. William, my arcane canine assistant, was busy talking to some customers about the difference between Moon Potion (a sleeping draught) and Moon Powder (very sparkly powdered rock). Safe in a quiet alcove of reference texts and empty bottles for sale, I continued ribbing Luca. "Looking for a catastrophe to avert? Sorry to tell you, we're fresh out of bottled danger."

Luca pulled his hood back, just a little, and grinned at me. Some of the weariness left him as he retorted, "You know as well as I do only fools go looking for danger, Red. If I wanted to prove myself, all I'd have to do is, say, venture into a haunted forest at night time . . ."

I held up two fingers, grinning back. "One, wasn't haunted, it was just a sorcerer, who by the way gave us a very pretty little statue because *some* of us have continued the search for horses while you're out saving the world, and two, I didn't have any choice in the matter, I was led there. What's your excuse? I heard you lifted the entire festival stage the other day to save a dragonling's tail."

"You found another horse and didn't tell me?" Luca settled against the wooden bookcase and leaned closer, his voice dropping as he glanced over his shoulder. I rolled my eyes.

"You've been a hard man to keep up with," I observed, dryly.

"Not unlike someone else I know!" With good humor, Luca snorted. "I tried to catch you at the store a few days ago but you were out with Officer Thorn."

"Catching bad guys. Jealous?"

"What—no! I never *meant* to be some kind of hero, Red. I was actually on my way here when it first happened. There was this self-driving cart barreling down the road and I was in a hurry and didn't notice it until it was right on top of me, and then, well . . ."

Seeing as it was apparently story time, I'd perched on the arm of a nearby comfy chair. Now I lifted an eyebrow and finished the sentence for him. "Your latent super powers awakened?"

"It's not super powers," he frowned at me. "It's *this*. This is what I was coming to see you about."

Luca reached toward his robe, where I could only imagine there were a number of pockets with who knows what inside them. Books and journals and half-used quills, probably. As I watched he flailed a bit then finally threw up his hands, grabbed a tome on minerals off the nearest shelf, and flopped into the chair I was leaning against.

"What in Beyond is wrong with you?" I asked, swiveling to keep him in my field of vision. "Stress of saving the town's young getting to be too much?"

"Hush, Red. You know exactly what it is." Luca propped the book up on his knees and, behind it, set a black statuette in his lap. "*This*."

"Huh. So you found one too." Despite my better judgment I pulled my alchemists' goggles down over my eyes and leaned in, stuffing my long black hair back over my shoulder so I could focus. Luca had brought in our sixth carousel horse. Like the others, it was only as high as my palm, prancing on a golden pole. But this one was a matte black—unpolished hematite ore, or even coal, in my opinion—and on it was carved an ornate bridle and saddle blanket, like the kind you would see on a knight's horse.

The knight symbolism might explain whatever charm is in it, I thought. *If it's giving Luca some kind of armor, that would make sense.*

And apparently it was necessary, if Luca was wandering the streets with his head in the clouds. Realizing suddenly that a lot worse could have happened to him—because danger went hand in hand with these little horses—I pulled back and narrowed my eyes.

"Where'd you find it?" I asked.

"Um, well," said Luca, in the tone of someone who's about to say "funny story" and make everyone with brains the opposite of amused.

"I *knew* it," I sighed. "There can't ever be anything straightforward with these. Out with it, then, come on!"

"It was just by this pile of rocks! I mean, that's what I thought at the time. I was taking out the trash for the store, and it was all just sitting there in the yard." Pursing my lips at the thought that Luca just accepted a random pile of rocks at the back of his store, I waited until he continued, "Aaand then this morning the pile of rocks was gone, and I saw Officer Thorn put out a notice for information about a dead person missing in the area . . . and I realized I really had waited too long to tell you."

With a sharp intake of breath, I cursed. Officer Thorn, magic horses, and dead rock trolls could only mean one thing. "*Lark.*"

* * *

Let me pause here for a moment to say that when I'd told Luca that Officer Thorn and I were out "catching bad guys," the one in charge of all those bad guys was Lark. She was the head of the nearest bad guy operation. The local boss, you might say.

I'm not saying *all* bad guys in Belville reported to her—the town had always had its share of passion crimes and ne'er-do-wells, and who knows what kind of out-of-towners had come in for the festival. Lark herself was from out of town, actually:

she was a coastal elf with a team of underlings. I knew this all because I'd been the one to help Officer Thorn find their hideout in a cave outside of town.

Since that initial encounter, Thorn had told me that Lark's organization had reportedly moved into town to mine for something or another to help build wheelchairs for kids. "Something or another" was Thorn's term, not mine. I had a healthy professional jealousy of whoever had put Lark's wheelchair together, so I wasn't going to quibble with Lark if she said that was her goal. But her methods, which so far had involved potential theft and murder of the local mailcarrier, left a lot to be desired.

Oh, and aside from being unscrupulous, she definitely employed rock trolls. I didn't have to be descended from a tribe of Seers to know exactly what Luca had gotten himself into.

* * *

"But exactly *how much* trouble? See, you can't say for sure!" Luca whispered triumphantly after I'd filled him in. By then other customers had filtered into the shop, and William was giving me dirty looks. I wanted to argue with Luca, but bit my tongue. He went on, "We don't know if the horses are important to Lark, or if Lark just happened to have them. That's why we need to investigate!"

"Has borrowing magic powers made you crazy?" My question came out more as a croak. "Weren't you *just* saying that only fools go looking for trouble?"

"Danger, but close." Luca grinned as he shifted to look up

at me squarely. The horse had long since disappeared into his pockets. "So what if it has? Why shouldn't we use them to help in the investigation? This is a really big lead, Red. Six horses have been found, which leaves only three. We're so close to the end—and don't you want to know what this has all been about?"

"I do not. And even if I did, I couldn't lead you back there anyway," I protested, meaning Lark's lair. Thorn and I had found it only because of a tracing charm.

Luca pressed his lips together and gave me a knowing look. "Red, you want answers even more than I do. You're never going to rest until you have them. And *I* know how to get there. I'm going to see what they have to do with these horses, whether you're coming or not."

"What—how—how do you know how to get there?"

"I had to make a delivery for the foreman," Luca explained cheerfully as he stood up. "He's a pretty cool guy, we bonded over talk about demanding bosses. So, we leave after closing up the shops this evening?"

I hesitated. But I had to admit he had me pegged, in at least one particular: there was no way I was letting a friend run off into danger alone. "Fine. But I've only got enough dinner cooking for one, so you better bring your own snacks."

* * *

It was precisely one minute after closing when Luca bounded up to the shop door once more. This time he was no longer Bookstore Clerk Luca, but Adventure Luca. I could tell because in addition to his robes he now carried a walking stick and gingham bundle tied neatly on top, like a small child's lunch.

"You do know this isn't a fieldtrip, right?" I asked him, laughing as I set aside my cleaning cloth.

Luca grinned from one edge of his hood to another. "Well it isn't battle either. What are you going to do, Red, poison anyone who looks at us funny?"

He gestured to what William refers to as my "nerd belt," which I'd donned over my tunic. In various pockets and clips rested numerous vials and ingredients—things I could use for far more than poisoning people. But also poisoning people, just in case.

"Listen, you may think we're just going to poke around for information, but I'm telling you these people are unfriendly. When Thorn and I went—"

"But Red, you haven't met Longbeard! He's the one I want to see. He'll know all about it and he's a nice guy who's just interested in—"

From above, William's voice broke in. "Must you two *always* argue? You're giving me a headache."

"Good thing you don't have to deal with us more than a moment, then," I reminded my assistant as he descended from our apartment into the shop. Once he was within reach, I grabbed my own hastily-packed dinner from his jaws.

Luca looked at William with interest. "You don't want to come along?"

"Go out into the forest with you two, probably get lost in the mountain somewhere, all because you can't stop playing with cursed toys?" William sneezed. "No thanks. I'm going to go hang out with the sorcerers at the Festival."

"Suit yourself," Luca shrugged, turning to me. "All set, then?

Let's go, daylight's wasting!"

And with one more eye roll from William, we were off. Luca led the way, parting the seas of Belville's busy evening streets with his ratty walking stick. Everyone—literally everyone, from the old fairy who sold golden eggs to the stringy armorer to the vampire florist who hadn't been known to smile in decades to Dusty, local plumber and handy-gnome, walking to work with a wrench over his shoulder—beamed at Luca as he went past. When we turned onto a sidestreet, headed for the hills south of town, I figured the blaze of public attention had faded enough that I could risk walking at his side.

"So," I began, looking down at the sandwich in my hand philosophically, "want to tell me again why it took you so long to give up the armored horse?"

"Is that what we're calling it?" Luca tilted his head to look at me, then leaned over to catch a glimpse of my mobile dinner. "Hey, I thought you said you were cooking?"

"Save your questions for Lark. Or—what was your friend's name?"

"Longbeard. You'll like him. Actually, you might not, since you're kind of similar. Anyway he's the one I made the delivery for, so he'll be able to tell us what's going on and what might have happened to the rock trolls and if they're really looking for carousel horses. Not that we should actually ask him that outright, of course, but—"

"Hold up," I said, having finally swallowed a large bite of bread and cress. "How am I similar to this pirate?"

"He isn't a pirate," Luca protested. "I mean, he does have a lot of tattoos, but I'm pretty sure all his limbs are accounted for. Unless he's got good prosthetics. Have you seen what the fae can do these days?"

"Don't remind me," I mumbled, thinking of Lark's wheelchair. "And can we focus, please?"

"On you, or on Longbeard?" Luca grinned as he veered off the sidestreet and through a lilac bush. Once we were past the undergrowth, I could see we were actually on a well-worn path winding into the trees around the corner of a hill.

"On where we're going," I insisted, jogging a little to keep up. "This isn't anything like the path Thorn and I took."

"Well, maybe you weren't going to the same place," said Luca with the kind of blithe rationality that made me want to throw the crust of my sandwich at his head. "This is where Longbeard told me to go when I was bringing the maps he'd ordered. It's just around the bend, here."

"What'd he want maps for?" I shoveled the rest of my dinner down, took a gulp from my flask, and took a good look around just in case Luca wasn't as sure of where we were as he said. Most of the town had already disappeared, beyond the trees and the hillside. The sky overhead was just the kind you want for summer festivals, cotton candy colors. But I still had a bad feeling.

"For this," Luca said, scrambling up a rockfall and turning a corner to look into a ravine. I followed, peering over his shoulder—in fact, nearly knocking him over as I skidded to a halt.

"Saints of the earth preserve us," I cursed under my breath. "I mean, sorry for almost knocking you over. But you could have warned me, Luca!"

There at the back of the ravine was what someone more poetic than me might have taken for one of the gates of hell. An opening big enough for a cart to pass through had been cut violently out of the dark rock. All plant life or anything living had been cleared away, leaving scorched earth. And inside that opening, rather than shadows and stalactites, an eerie red glow pulsed.

"You wouldn't have believed me." Luca sidled self-consciously—*as well he should,* I thought. He added, "Anyway, that's not what matters. We're here to find Longbeard, remember? He should be somewhere in the camp there by the cliff."

"Oh, you mean, right in front of the active and angry mining site?"

"Well, 'angry' might be taking a liberty, don't you think? And I thought alchemists liked mines—"

"Not this one! There is something *wrong* here."

"I'm going," Luca declared, thrusting his walking stick into the dirt. "And if you're coming, I suggest you don't say stuff like that to our hosts."

"Hosts, or potential murderers?" But I merely muttered the words as I followed Luca. He stepped carefully, clutching at roots, until finally giving up and sliding down the side of the ravine to get to the camp at the bottom. Camp—that'd been his word: I myself would have called it an evil villain's trash heap. Bits of twisted iron, probably the remains of old minecarts, were strewn about carelessly. A few haphazard tents reclined against the cliff face, while a shed surrounded by a ring of discarded tools owned the scene like a watchful dragon. The entire place reeked like a giant's sweaty shoe.

There wasn't anyone visible in camp, though there were regular sounds of picks and hammers coming from the mine. As we hopped over a set of tracks running straight into that gaping maw, I wondered if maybe it wasn't a mine at all. But I didn't have time to follow up that thought, because Luca was about to stride right into the shed.

Now, I get that most people don't consider alchemists' goggles to be a savvy fashion choice. (William isn't the only one who's called me a nerd.) But in my world function rules over form, and that's one of the reasons I'm never without mine. I'd pulled my goggles over my head as we descended into the ravine to get a closer look at the rubble and tools. Not that I'm one to brag, but I made them specially with something called "Souled Glass" which can sense where I'm looking and—well, to spare you all the technical details, I'll just say the zoom is variable. And very, very strong.

Because I still had my goggles on, I saw what Luca didn't: the flash of not one knife but two shining through the cracks in the hastily-built shed. On impulse I leapt forward, once more tackling Luca from behind—this time on purpose, though. Before he could step into some kind of knife fight, I tugged him into the deep shadow between the shed and the cliff.

"Hey, what gives? Let—"

"Shut up," I hissed, releasing my grip on Luca's shoulders only when I was sure he'd stay hidden. As quickly as I could, I explained what I'd seen.

"You think they're fighting each other?" Luca's hooded head tilted as he thought about it. "Then they won't notice if I go up for a closer look."

"Luca! Did you forget the part where I just dragged you *away* from the murder shack?"

"You know," whispered Luca, glancing over his shoulder, "it's not nice to make assumptions about others. And don't worry, I'm a lot sneakier than you think."

I have to admit, I doubted it. But call me a hack and a peddler if he didn't prove me wrong.

Luca might as well have been gliding over the dark ground as he moved toward the shed, for all the noise he made. He crouched as he moved up to the wall and placed himself beneath a half-boarded-over window. No one inside could see him, and anyone moving through camp would have had to come all the way around the shack to notice he was there.

Duly impressed, I followed suit. As we knelt together in the dirt, our ears straining to catch sounds from inside the shack, I heard snippets of conversation:

"—that's *another* one gone. How many—"

"—he was going against Lark's orders—"

Thunk "But the work must get done!"

". . . find a way around it . . ."

". . . know what happens to people who take matters into their own hands."

Somebody's knife made a *shiiing* sound and I shivered. Luca turned one eye on me. "Don't worry," he whispered once more. "They were putting it back in a sheath, I think."

"Either way, I doubt they want to answer your questions," I murmured back.

Luca shifted to face me, leaning on the wall. "Maybe they already have. The 'other one gone' could be the carousel horse. Of course, it could also be the rock—"

From somewhere near the cliff face, something very big scraped over the ground. As one, Luca and I turned to see a form detach itself from the ravine. First one—then another. Rock trolls.

"But that's impossible," said Luca, forgetting himself. "That's—that's the one that was dead behind the bookshop!"

"We can talk about it later!" I insisted, throwing my hand on his arm to get him to be quiet. My mind raced. I couldn't remember: could rock trolls hear well? See well? Could they smell us sitting here in the shadow?

One of the hulking forms, each as big as the shack we were cowering against, pivoted toward the other. "Oh look, Skar."

"Yes, Skaab?"

Great, I thought, watching them rumble closer as they continued their polite conversation. *These are definitely the two from Lark's luncheon the other day.*

Skaab's luminescent moss beard glowed, lighting up one great arm as it pointed to Luca. "That's the snitch. The one the foreman told."

"In that case," said Skar, tiny eyes burning, "perhaps we ought to tie up loose ends."

"Luca," I hissed under my breath, "I'm really starting to get the feeling that it wasn't a rock troll that was killed."

"But in the yard behind the shop—"

"Was that the same day Longbeard came to you? Did you ever think that maybe Officer Thorn's missing-presumed-dead person was *him,* and not the rock troll at all?"

"You're probably right. Curse it!" Luca began looking around. With the shack at our backs and the ravine in front of us and the rock trolls within lunging distance, we didn't have much choice. "Run!"

Like some kind of four-legged, two-headed creature, both Luca and I scrambled side by side to the left, out toward the mouth of the ravine. The teals and blues of the twilight sky were visible high above us, a tantalizing opposite of everything we'd encountered in the camp. But that open sky was far away, blocked by rocks and tents and dark towering trees. It felt like the hillsides were closing in. I grabbed Luca's wrist, ready to pull him along with me in a desperate sprint. But just as I had the idea, new sounds and shapes appeared in front of us.

I, I am proud to say, properly identified the new obstacle—"Kitchen caravan!"—while Luca merely yelped like a startled child.

I had to think quickly. Skar and Skaab weren't close yet, but they weren't stopping, either. The caravan had several carts and at least half a dozen attendants, ready to set up dinner for the miners. A dinner that probably came with lots of knives and pots of boiling liquid and, in general, nothing I wanted to deal with personally. "Come on!" I cried, yanking at Luca. "Only one way left!"

And with that, I hurtled us both back toward the gaping hole in the mountain. Those tracks we had crossed earlier flew by under my feet as I ran. And there, right at the tunnel entrance, a cart stood in our way. Without thinking I flung both of us into it and, powered by our momentum, it began rattling downward into the mountain's depths.

"How is this any better?" Luca sputtered, struggling to right himself. His legs were tangled in his robes which were getting under my feet in the minecart, which was no bigger than a bale of hay. He had to yell to be heard over the clanging rails, the din of mining, and the *whoosh* of air going past us as the cart picked up speed. And—was that Skar and Skaab, still yelling behind us? "You have no idea where this goes!"

"I don't know, I panicked!" I admitted. Seeing some very confused and unfriendly miners along the edges of the tunnel ahead, I shoved Luca's head down just as he had gotten himself upright. "I hate enclosed spaces," I moaned as we hurtled past the miners. A few brandished hammers over our heads, but fortunately none thought of stopping the cart.

Then the tracks dipped into a steep incline down a very dark tunnel, and I wondered if we'd been fortunate or not.

"Really? Because this seems like the definition of a confined space," Luca said. In the gloom all I could see were his green eyes and the glint of the cart behind his shoulder. The ceiling above us was so close I could have reached out and touched it, if I had wanted to lose a few fingers at the rate we were going.

"I don't want to talk about it," I decided, shutting my eyes.

The tunnel opened up into a cavern and red light assaulted my eyes, making it impossible to keep them shut. I looked around wildly to see we were speeding through some kind of natural cave, lined with a mineral we passed too fast for me to identify, filled with an unearthly heat. At least, it sure felt hot to me—even with the constant rush of wind—and I don't think it's because I'm *that* much of a scaredy cat. Luca must have felt it too, both the heat and the worry. As the tracks jerked us mercilessly up and down and side to side, his hand found mine.

"Hold this with me," he shouted, and I realized he'd brought out the armored horse. "Maybe it will protect us both!"

It ought to, it's the reason we're here in the first place, I thought giddily, almost relieved when the cart dove back into a black tunnel. A hard right turn brought my head much closer to an outcrop of pegmatite granite than I ever want to be in my life.

"Look ahead!" Luca tugged at my arm. "I think I see lights!"

All I *really* wanted to do was duck my head inside the cart and not look at anything until the ride was over. But he was right—there was light, not red but a mossy green, and beyond it a hint of silver that suggested the moon. The cart bumped and jostled and slowed as we passed tunnels that criss-crossed our own—tunnels I recognized.

"Lark," I told Luca incoherently. I tried again. "This is Lark's place—keep your voice down!"

Luca's eyes widened and he nodded. The cart glided past the tunnels and out into the open air at last. Then it lurched to a gut-clenching halt and both Luca and I screamed.

"Arr, look what we have here."

Sprawled on my back on the ground in a small clearing, I looked up at the man who'd thrown the brakes on our cart. Beside me, Luca cried out,

"Longbeard! Oh, good thing. We were worried you were dead."

And then the pirate—because really, how could Luca not have known he was a pirate?—stepped back, and the light hit his face. His grayed, almost greenish face. My hand went instantly to my potion belt as I sat up.

Oh dear, I thought. I had *not* been prepared for a roller coaster ride, nor for dealing with creatures from the other side. *What do I have that might stop—*

"Dead?" The pirate Longbeard laughed, long and hard. "Aye, that I am, son. I knew they had it out for me. They're after me gold! I got one o' them sorcerers to whip up a spell for me, somethin' to bring me back, seein' as I'm always one step ahead. I beat 'em at their own game!"

"You're *dead?*" Luca sounded amazed. "So it *was* you that got set up? But we were coming to see you! I was hoping you could tell me—"

"Arr," said the pirate. "I'm not telling anyone nothing. An' I don't think I want you hangin' round any more."

So saying, zombie-Longbeard drew a long curved sword and stabbed down toward Luca. But Luca dodged it quickly, almost as though he wasn't winded from the minecart's abrupt end—and of course he wasn't, I realized. Because he was still holding the armored horse.

"Why is that?" panted Luca. When the pirate only cackled, he guessed, "Because you're worried I'll show your old coworkers the maps you wanted? The maps of mineral deposits right where they think they're building a railroad?"

I saw at once what Luca was doing. He wanted to keep Longbeard occupied, so that I could—what? My fingers raced over my belt as I took stock. Flash Powder? No, that wouldn't work. The Miraculous Melting Lock Pick? No good here. Containment vials? The last thing I wanted was a sample of this cursed dead dude. Confusement Potion? Did zombies even have brains to confuse? *Statue Powder—that might work,* I realized. It was drastic, but if a cutlass-wielding undead pirate didn't call for drastic, I don't know what did.

I climbed unsteadily to my feet and began advancing on Longbeard, who was turned away from me, hacking at Luca and hitting dirt. The last thing I wanted was to hit Luca, too. I started waving my arms over my head, trying to get him to understand the danger. *Get out of there,* I was trying to say.

He stared back at me over Longbeard's shoulder as if to reply, *You think I'm not trying that already?*

"Hey, pirate," I said aloud, tiring of subterfuge. "I have something even better than gold for you, right here!"

Longbeard turned, more surprised than anything else. My arms were already upraised, ready to sprinkle the powder over him and turn him into a terrible piece of art.

But nothing happened.

I realized in a panic that the vial stopper wasn't opening. The cork was supposed to be powder-proof. Was it really going to fail me now? Just when I had given up yanking at it and was about to simply smash the vial on the pirate's head, I looked up to realize he wasn't there.

And that's when the sound hit me. With a violent, ripping thunder, Skar and Skaab had emerged from the (now considerably wider) tunnel. They'd rushed past me and now the pirate lay squished under them both.

"Wait," I said to no one in particular. "Where's Luca?"

"Here," came the muffled cry from below two heaps of rock. "I guess . . . it's a good thing . . . I brought the horse along, huh?"

* * *

Once they had picked themselves up and well-meaningly, if clumsily, dusted Luca off, Skar and Skaab explained that they only cared about Luca and me if we were working with Longbeard. Which, given that I had been about to poison him and he had been trying to gut Luca, the rock trolls could agree that we weren't.

Longbeard had been the last in a series of foremen to "go wrong," as Skar put it sadly. None could seem to focus on building the railroad Lark required; they all got distracted by things like "digging into a new dimension" and, of course, looking for gold. Choosing not to reflect on what it was about mining that seemed to make people crazy, Skaab instead ended the conversation on a high note, remarking that try as they might, no one could stand in the way of progress.

As Luca and I made our way home, I couldn't help but reflect that "progress" made my head spin.

"So you're telling me," said William, when at last I was curled up in my bed and had finally caught him up on all that had happened, "they just said 'thanks for helping us catch a zombie' and let you walk off with a magical horse that'll take you to hell?"

"I'm sorry, it'll what now?"

"Well, that's what it *should* do," William corrected himself. His tail thumped, shaking the entire mattress from his place at the end of the bed. We'd already put away the armored horse, safe with the others, but I could tell he'd been longing to talk about it. "It's obviously a *cheval mallet*. Kind of like a kelpie, but it won't take you underwater, if you catch my drift. Maybe it's what was making the miners crazy, somehow."

"I don't know, none of the other horses have had that kind of effect," I mused.

William shook his floppy ears. "Maybe you just haven't noticed because you're already nuts."

"Har har!" I threw a throw pillow at him. (It's what they're for, isn't it?) "Anyway, that's all well and good, but we already know what this horse's power is. It was giving Luca armor, remember? Otherwise he would've been pulverized."

I gulped a little upon realizing that fact, and William snorted. "There's another who's crazy already. And he just packed up and went home none the worse for his adventure, eh?"

"Well . . ." I blushed. Actually, Luca had been pretty exuberant on the way home, as had I. After all, we'd just escaped death three or four times over, and Skar and Skaab seemed to have forgotten all about the horse, so the evening felt like a win-win. Luca'd been full of annoyingly true things to say, like how he'd known from the beginning I'd be up for an investigation simply because I was an alchemist. *And he goes around telling other people not to make assumptions!*

"Well what?"

"Oh." I shook myself, and then yawned. "He's none the worse than he ever is, at least. And neither am I. So you don't have to worry."

"Who said I was worried? Crazy kids. What's it going to be for the next horse? A haunted maze? A cursed ghost ship? A pyramid full of mummies and spiders?"

"Goodnight, William," I said loudly in response. As I flopped down in bed, I couldn't help chuckling. William was right to point out the danger; I was well aware of that. Each horse *did* seem to get a little more ludicrous than the last.

Truthfully, I was starting to enjoy the challenge. But I hadn't forgotten that, according to people much more mystical than me, these little horses could ruin the world.

I had a feeling it would take more than superpowers to figure this mess out—but that, I decided, was a problem for tomorrow.

7

A Fiery Depth

The Seventh Carousel Caper

It started as a normal murder. I know, that's pretty much the worst thing you could say when murder's involved. But my life in small-town Belville had become a string of *abnormal* encounters, each wilder than the last—as you're about to see.

That particular morning, Officer Thorn, local police officer and owner of the smartest collection of suits in all Pastoria, strode into my alchemy shop the moment I unlocked the door. We were entering the fourth and final week of the pixies' month-long sorcerer-themed festival, and I had only just gotten used to the rush of business. I met the Officer with caffeine-fueled cheerfulness—only to find, upon closer inspection, that she was decidedly disheveled and un-cheery.

"Good morning, Off—"

"Red! I need a truth potion."

I blinked at her, in part because she hadn't done her usual salute and warning cry of "Officer Thorn reporting!". But also because, in the season since I'd begrudgingly begun working with her as an unofficial assistant, I hadn't realized that we needed to have this discussion. "No," I managed after a minute, my hands on my hips.

"What? What do you mean, 'no'?" Officer Thorn waved one large, green-skinned hand at the surrounding shelves, some climbing the walls and others clustered into themed displays, all bearing potion bottles and various ingredients. "You must have *something* of use in here!"

"I have many things of use," I retorted—defensively, I'll admit. "But I do *not* carry truth potions."

"Then make one. This is a matter of murder—"

"I said *no,*" I repeated, raising my voice since she clearly wasn't listening. "Do you even know what you're asking? A truth potion'd take ages to prepare, plus it would need to be started under the new moon, which isn't due for days. All of which is moot because I'm just. Not. Doing it!"

There was a pause—most likely, Officer Thorn was trying to decide if she'd have more luck getting the answer she wanted if I was in handcuffs (the answer still would have been no). In that pause, the door to my apartment on the shop's second floor opened, and William—shaggy black beauty-sleep-deprived familiar—shuffled out on to the spiral staircase and gave us a doggy glare.

"Red's a Seer," he told Thorn, his voice so gruff it was almost hard to understand. "They don't take truth lightly out there in the desert, you know."

Officer Thorn stuttered, her purple eyes wide. "B-but I

thought—"

"Am not," I declared, as though I was four and had been labeled a "stupid-head." "Of course I'm not. Don't listen to him. He told you once I was a swamp warrior, remember? You can never trust anything he says."

"She doesn't even know how to make truth potions," William continued loudly, sitting down to watch us with a resounding *thump.*

"I do, but I won't," I insisted to Thorn. "Listen, it's like this. You just have to come up with another method of finding out what you want. I'll help you find evidence, but I'm not going to be an accessory to coercion."

Officer Thorn tapped a fingernail against one very long canine as she thought. "Fine," she said at last, stepping aside so some early-morning shoppers—more like curious gossips wanting to know why there was yelling coming from my shop, but such is life—could enter. "But in that case you're going to have to come see the victim, over at the station. Do an inspection, like you did last time."

"No problem," I assured her, only grinding my teeth a little. Looking up over my shoulder, I cast William a *we're going to be talking later* glower. "William, since you're up so early, why don't you come down and help out our customers? I'll be back before long."

* * *

No doubt by the time Officer Thorn and I made it across town to her little station, the entire countryside had heard the rumors of murder. Blissfully unaware of the talk, I set down my travel bag of tools and strode at once to the victim, laid out in Thorn's back room.

It was definitely murder, all right. I tallied up other facts as I looked over the body: deep green skin and webbing between the fingers and toes. No clothes—only a swimming costume, and part of the strap of a water-logged messenger bag. A ring of mother-of-pearl and an amber pendant on a necklace. Long brown hair, pointy ears, and rough, dark strangulation marks on the neck.

"Went by Finn," Officer Thorn told me from the door. "Half merfolk, half elf. Just a boy, really. Been here a few years earning a living doing water spells and underwater work as needed. Some shepherds found him down by Lake Lava last night when they went to water their flocks."

"Found him where, exactly?" I asked.

"On the shore. Half in, half out—feet still in the water. Did you know half-merfolk get fins in water?"

I shook my head at Thorn's abrupt departure from "stern police woman" to "student of the world." I didn't know much about merfolk at all, but I did know that if Finn's wounds hadn't been underwater, I might be able to help more easily than I'd thought.

Calming the queasiness in my stomach, I swept my own long hair over my shoulder and leaned down for a closer look. Tugging my alchemists' goggles from my forehead down over my eyes, I examined the bruises on Finn's neck. The coloring was painful and dark—the darkness camouflaging what I'd hoped to find: traces of mud and other residues.

"Alright, here's my first idea," I said as I stood back up. "In my bag I've got some earth-aspected affinity powder. It reacts with different lights to different minerals and metals. If we use a few pinches of that on the residues on Finn's neck, maybe we can pick up extra clues."

"Like what?" Thorn asked, not stirring as she watched me pull out a glass jar and scoop, as well as a clean white cloth. "Specific kinds of dirt?"

"Yeah, but more importantly, it might help us notice some things there that *aren't* dirt," I said. "If we can single out any anomalies, they'll probably be of more help than any dirt or sand. I'm not saying this will solve the case—it might not do anything—but it's a place to start."

"I like the way you think, assistant," Officer Thorn declared with a toothy grin. Behind her, there was a faint magical siren as someone opened the front door of the station. "And here's my main suspect, come in for his interview. Save some of that powder stuff for his hands, won't you?"

"What?" I jerked in surprise, nearly smudging my own experiment. I hadn't realized Thorn had a suspect already—though her desperation for truth potions probably should have tipped me off. I also had never heard of a murderer willingly reporting to the police station.

"No time for 'whats'," she informed me. "We'll be in my office. You come over when you're done."

"That really wasn't the point of using the affinity powder," I mumbled, knowing that she'd already gone but unwilling to let my opposition go unvoiced. "I'm not here to analyze the cursed dirt."

And yet, it turned out, I was. Try as I might, four repetitions of my experiment all showed the same result: *nothing* in the smears from Finn's neck was unnatural. That would have shown with a quick black flash: all I was getting, time and again, was a steady purple burn (shale), sparks of white (iron), and a gold glow (kaolin).

When I went to Thorn to report this, preparing myself to insist that *yes, I'd tested my powder on the man-made strands of Finn's pendant just to be sure it did work,* I found her deep in a staring match with an absolute hulk of a suspect.

"Ah, there's our alchemist," Thorn said the moment I opened the door to her immaculate office. She glared pointedly at her interviewee, as though alchemists were known to be great weapons of the judicial system. I suppose a few unscrupulous ones have, but even more haven't. "Red, this is . . . Knee."

"Knee?" I repeated incredulously, looking at a mass of shoulders and arm muscles.

"'S a nickname." As he turned I could see him better: knobby ears and rust-red tinted skin that spoke of ogre heritage, and eyes deeply wrinkled. But his voice was young. "The dwarves couldn't never say my old one."

"I . . . see." *His old name, not his real name,* I observed. Still, who was I to judge anyone for changing their name? I pulled myself together and informed Officer Thorn that we'd need to try another idea. I'd got about one tenth of the way through my explanation when she interrupted.

"Purple, white, gold glow," she rattled off. "Perfect. Let's see what this one's got on his hands, shall we?"

"Officer, really," I protested. Knee said nothing. "What makes you think that—"

"It's just a little test," she continued.

"Doesn't he have to consent, at least?"

She narrowed her eyes at Knee. "He'd better."

Knee looked up at me. "It won't hurt, will it?"

"No, it won't." I sighed, figuring I'd get it over with and argue with Thorn later.

Which is exactly what I found myself doing, thirty minutes later, when Thorn had Knee locked up in the basement because of a purple glow with white specks.

"It's not conclusive," I repeated. We were back in her office, alone, and by that point I was wondering if I was speaking the right language. "Shale and iron are common around here. There could be any number of reasons—"

"—and one of those could be murder!"

"It just as well might not be! How about we go around and test everyone's hands, then? Mine would probably give the same result. Heck, even someone completely harmless who just happens to work with their hands, like Dusty, would be the same," I said, exasperated. I brought up my friend not to incriminate him—as local handy-gnome, he was far too helpful to be locked away, for one thing—but to point out how ridiculous this all was.

Thorn brought her fist down on her ponderous desk like *I* was the unruly one. "I just need him to break, Red. Just give it time and he'll confess. It's what they always do!"

"Excuse me? Who is '*they*'?"

"You know. Murderers," she explained, tossing her head. "This kind, anyway. Take it from me, this was a crime of passion. Knee and Finn were involved, did you know that? Said they met through friends who *knit.* Now those friends report they've been fighting—"

I scoffed. "What counts as fighting to a knitter? Tug-of-war?"

"I didn't bring you here to be funny, Red. Don't . . . Don't . . . oh, curse it," said Thorn, and broke out into a belly-laugh that even poor Knee in his cell could probably hear. "That was a good one, I'll give you that. But don't you go making a simple case complicated. It's just two young people, finding their way in the world, then one gets ahead of the other and the other gets jealous. Tragic, yes. Mysterious, no."

"I'll give you that I can see why they were drawn together," I conceded. "They're clearly two people between worlds. But is this really all you have to go on? What about the lake—why was Finn out there in the first place?"

"Word is, he was diving there on commission yesterday."

"Commission from who?"

"No one could say, but supposedly it was to look for earthen vessels, or something. But no one saw him after he left that morning—so they say, in any case. I scoured that beach last night, and there weren't any prints but the shepherds', Finn's—and Knee's."

"So we know all we can from the crime scene. But," I said, sitting up in my chair, "what if something happened *in* the lake? You haven't looked there."

"Oh, no," rumbled Thorn, eyeing me suspiciously. "Don't tell me you have some potion that's going fix it so I breathe underwater."

"Actually," I said, standing and already picturing exactly where in my lab I'd need to go, "I do."

* * *

Lake Lava isn't a deathly pool of magma. It doesn't have anything to do with volcanoes or molten rock at all. I suppose it's possible that the lake is in the collapsed crater of an old volcano—Belville *is* on a mountain, after all—but for knowledge like that, we'd have had to check with the scholars at the bookstore. Word from Luca was that Owl was very upset about something (most likely a scroll shelved out of place) so I was giving the place a wide berth. I just figured everyone called the calm, deep blue lake "Lake Lava" because they liked the way it sounded.

Morning in Officer Thorn's office had felt like it stretched over eons, but it felt like a mere instant later that we found ourselves on the beach.

"This is the place," said Thorn as we stood on the sand and looked out at the tree-rimmed waters. "It's a popular spot for swimming. Most of the fishers prefer the old harbor further down."

I nodded, looking at the multitude of footprints around us. In my time at Belville, I hadn't yet been out to the lake. I am from the desert, after all; the musty, cold-dew smell of Lake Lava was enough to put me off. But, I reminded myself, we had a job to do.

"Here," I said, handing Thorn a vial from my bag and extracting my own vial before making sure all the waterproof latches were firmly pinned back down. "Drink up."

"*Yuck*," said Thorn, who'd made the mistake of sniffing her potion heartily before knocking it back. "Couldn't you just have given me a lakeweed to chew, or something?"

"That's an old myth. And anyway, would you rather put all your faith in *one* ingredient, or a cocktail of three?" Grinning, I showed her how it's done. I plugged my nose with one hand and downed the entire contents of the vial in one swig. "It's not so bad."

Thorn did as I did, coughed, and burped. "Well, I'll be. You were right. Tastes like . . . coconuts?"

"And vanilla," I said, kicking off my shoes. The leather would only weigh me down.

"Coconuts and vanilla's what makes people breathe under-water?"

"You think I'm going to give away my secrets so easily?" I laughed at the officer and—before I lost my mettle—ran into the water and dove as deep as I could.

I realized pretty quickly that Lake Lava was determined to out-deep "as deep as I could." The sandy bottom of the beach dropped away from us, as though a magician had swept away his magic carpet to reveal something much scarier than a rabbit or a dove. The lake walls were steep and dark. The water itself was the same clear blue it had appeared above, but the light sifting through the moving ripples over our heads made everything look like it was reflected by a fun-house mirror. Huge shadows rose up around Thorn and me, and I was struck by how *tiny* the average humanoid is when their legs and arms are just dangling around them.

The potion I'd grabbed for Thorn and myself was called Drowning Potion—not that I'd told her that. Really, it was the opposite of drowning. We could breathe underwater, but we could also move through it more easily. I tried to demonstrate this to Thorn, but it took her a while to catch on. She was clearly as excited about swimming as I had been (which was not).

At my shop, despite the constant distraction that was William, I'd also had the presence of mind to grab each of us an Ever-burning Lamp. So there I was, suspended in Lake Lava's depths, holding my little lamp in one hand and watching Thorn's blue light bob behind me, when I blinked and understood that the rock I'd been swimming toward was, in fact, the roof of a house.

I stopped dead in the water and thought through it again. Steep, angled, flat surface. Repeating, shingle-like pattern. Nice even ledge at the end. None of that added up to "rock," no matter how much I wanted it to.

When Thorn caught up with me, I gestured to my find, bewildered. She studied it soundlessly, her head tilted to one side. Finally my curiosity got the better of my common sense.

"What is it?" I asked aloud, even though I knew the water would distort the sound. Thorn furrowed her brow at me, and I all but shouted the question to get her to understand it.

She looked at the roof, then at me. "*House,*" she mouthed, her face eerie in the light of the lamps.

"I *know* that," I replied, frustrated. "But what is it doing here? I said—WHAT—IS—"

RAWWWWWWR.

For an instant I thought Lake Lava itself was tired of my stupid questions. But then a black form rocketed out from the blurry edges of my vision and collided with Thorn. That's when I realized it wasn't just fish keeping us company. My shouting had got us the attention of something much, much bigger.

Wordlessly—because sure, I make mistakes, but I try not to make the same one twice—I propelled myself towards Thorn, trying to untangle her from our attacker. *Huge fish—lake monster—shark—dragon?* My mind ran through the possibilities, each less likely than the next. When I got close I took hold of Thorn's arm and brought my lantern close to the creature. I'd hoped to find its face, to scare it off with the light. But all I saw in the struggle was what looked like an arm, and a leg, and skin made out of armored plates.

I kicked out at any appendage I could find and somehow,

Officer Thorn got herself free. The creature disappeared around the edge of the house. Thorn sank, clearly dazed, so I knew I had to do something. But what? I did have a dagger, not to mention my alchemy pack, but I doubted anything I had would make an impression on skin like armor plates. Not without a more detailed plan than "stab or throw potion then run." The creature reemerged over the roof, thrashing, its body shorter and thicker than I'd thought at first. Any minute, it was going to dive at us.

Of course at that moment my mind went blank.

And in that blankness, something called me from inside the house.

I went immediately, dragging Thorn behind me. She was heavy and not at all aerodynamic, but I went anyway, moving like I'd been caught in a tractor beam. One way or another I managed to pull her down beneath the roofline, find a doorway, wrench the rotted wood open, push Thorn inside, then slam the door in the creature's face. Fortunately, the rotted wood was banded by slightly-less-rotted iron. I locked the door on impulse, even though I didn't think for a moment it'd keep the creature out for long.

BOOM. BOOM.

Sure enough, the creature was rattling the entire cabin, trying to get in. Thorn had her hands to her head, getting her bearings. She'd lost her lamp. I shone mine around the room, searching desperately for inspiration. The floor was littered with unusable things, the last and heaviest remnants of whoever had lived here. But there, in the corner, I spied a trunk.

CRaaaaCK.

The sound through the water was muffled, but so strange it

sent a shiver down my spine that had me darting into the corner. Thorn was squaring off with the creature, which had ripped the door from its ancient hinges. Not unlike our attacker, I tore at the trunk, lobbing wood and a heavy iron lock over my shoulder. The moment a hole opened up, I plunged my hand in.

And found exactly what I'd been afraid of. Another cursed carousel horse.

I didn't care at all what it looked like or how it'd got there. By now, having found half a dozen of the things already, I knew how the gig worked. All I wanted was to find out what this particular horse's charm was. I prayed to every deity I could think of that it was a useful one.

Just something to help us get rid of the creature, I thought, grasping the horse. *Something to destroy it or help us get away. Please!*

"Oi!" Through the water I heard Officer Thorn cry out, and realized that I'd squeezed my eyes shut. Startled, I opened them. The room was filled with a golden glow—a glow coming from the horse, emanating between the cracks in my fingers. And pulsing off the creature that had attacked us as it disintegrated on the floor.

* * *

"I swear to you, William. It was *big,*" I insisted.

"Huge," Officer Thorn agreed, gesturing widely with both hands.

"Uh huh." William snuffled, turning a suspicious and beady gaze between the two of us. "This is starting to sound like a fishing story."

I glanced at Thorn. We were safe in my apartment, each wrapped in layers of towels, which didn't do much to argue our case. "It wasn't a fish! It was—it was—"

"A golem." William flopped down on the sofa, as though depressed by the weight of always knowing all the answers. "Yeah, yeah, yeah."

"A golem?" Thorn looked confused.

But the more I thought about it, the more it made sense. "I *did* see arms and legs, which must have meant it was humanoid . . ."

"Humanoid indeed! I got the marks to prove it," said Thorn, reshuffling her towels to show us. "It had its hands round my throat."

"Right," said William, "because you were trespassing."

"But if the horse's power is making this murderous golem, why can't we make it do that again?"

"Do we *want* to make it do that again?" Thorn muttered.

I rolled my eyes good-naturedly. "It's called repeatability, and it's the basis of any good experiment."

"So try it," William said, sitting up to pay attention.

I leaned over my tiny coffee table and picked up the horse in my hands. It didn't look at all like I'd expected. Somehow the image I'd had in my mind, back in the lake, was all dark earth and gold glow. But the horse itself was a serene blue and white—a beautiful example of porcelain, actually.

When I focused, I could feel the charm on the horse sparking and moving, like water—or more accurately, like magma. It was warm, almost hot. Then in a flash it was done, and there was a golem standing on my table, covered in plates of molten rock. Plates about the size of my fingernail. The entire thing was only as tall as the carousel horse.

William sneezed, then wuffed, then finally laughed aloud. After a moment, Thorn joined him.

"I don't think it's very funny," I observed, "seeing as I think *this* should be your murder suspect, Officer. After all, shale and iron—*and* kaolin, since the horse is porcelain, and I bet you the golem is too, and porcelain is made of kaolin—so all the traces I found on Finn could easily have come from that golem!"

"Oh, it's definitely the murderer," William agreed, sobering slightly. "I'll tell you what I think. Not that you asked. The horse is Qilin. It's an old Chinese legend—a horse that came from the center of the earth. So—"

"So it makes things out of earth," I said, unable to help myself beating William to the point occasionally. Fascinated, I reached out and poked the little golem on the table.

"Fine then. If you know everything already, explain the size," William challenged. When Thorn and I were quiet, he shook his floppy ears and continued, "That's the size the statue can make on its own, that little guy there. But if someone powerful had the horse, a real sorcerer, they could amplify that magic to make a bigger one. So," he continued, tail wagging, "there's some sorcerer out there—or *was* some sorcerer out there—who's your real murderer. That, or whoever sent the merfolk dude down into the lake."

I frowned at William. "How do you figure that?"

"Wait," said Thorn, clutching at her towels, deep in thought. "Actually, that might make sense. Some sort of earthenware, Finn was sent down there for . . . but I'd never heard of anyone getting pottery out of the lake . . ."

"See," said William. "Either the person sent Finn down there on purpose, knowing about the golem and what would happen. Or they didn't know what would happen, and just wanted that horse." His nose tipped down as he looked at the galloping horse on the table. "The horse which *you* now have, Red."

I didn't say anything. I wasn't worried—not exactly. We had wards up, William and I, and we had the other horses hidden. We'd always known there were other people who had wanted them. And just as I'd said to Thorn earlier, whoever was after these horses wasn't about to reveal all their secrets at once.

"Well," said Thorn, clapping a hand on the table with force enough to shatter the tiny golem. "Sounds like you two had better be careful, which I know you already are. And it sounds like I'd better go let a boy out of jail."

"Finally," I amended her statement as she grinned, and took her leave. Say what you will about Officer Thorn; she's surprisingly graceful about admitting when she's been wrong.

"Seven down, two to go," William observed once we were alone. His black fur glowed faintly with starry blue light. "What was it? When all nine are together, they can be powerful enough to destroy the world?" He sneezed. "With all the sorcerers around here, this is bound to get serious. We really need to find out who our competition is, Red."

"This has been serious the whole time," I protested, but in my heart I knew that William was right. What had begun as a "normal murder"—in fact, what had begun nearly a month ago as a little carousel horse trinket from a friend showing up in the mail—was about to get very serious, indeed.

8

A Stony Game

The Eighth Carousel Caper

I 'm a scientist. I don't *do* games. William—the arcane dog-familiar whose primary mode is "grumpy"—calls me "as fun as a block of stone." *He*'s all about games, probably because it's so contrary to what one would expect of him. And also because games of any stripe are a chance for him to show off how smart he is. Gambling, racing, fairy chess, magitech jenga, you name it—he's all over it.

Except when the pixies are the ones running the game.

Which in small-town Belville, they usually are.

But this particular adventure didn't start with pixies or fun of any sort. Actually, I set out that day to tie up loose ends in an ongoing murder investigation. A few days before, a half-elf-half-merfolk boy named Finn had been found strangled at the edge of Lake Lava (no actual lava involved). Officer

Thorn, brash and stubborn as always, had determined that the murderer was the boy's lover, an ogre-ish sort who went by the name Knee. The actual culprit had turned out to be an ancient curse carried by a tiny carousel horse with the more imaginative name Qilin. But curses—and cursed carousel horses, with which I had become reluctantly familiar—don't act on their own. Someone, I knew, had sent Finn down into the lake and got him killed, whether on purpose or not. And since Thorn had no leads and no amount of ghost-work could contact Finn, I was helping out with a bit of legwork.

Let's be clear: I am not, I repeat *not,* a police officer of any stripe. In fact I am the daughter of Seers and a practicing alchemist, a former traveler and current shop owner, and really everything as far from the law as you can get without actually being illegal. But the moment I'd stepped foot in Belville, Officer Thorn had decided I'd make the perfect "unofficial assistant." I'd never been able to protest successfully. Much like I'd never been able to stop tripping over cursed carousel horses, nor able to live up to William's standard of "fun."

And so, that was why I was using my morning off to interview a rock.

That's what it felt like, at least. I'd found Knee in a local mine and patiently waited for him to go on break. But now as he and I sat there, him about twice as tall and four times as wide as me as he hunched on the end of a broken minecart as far from me as he could possibly be, I realized that he was doing the exact same thing. Patiently waiting out my attempts at conversation until it was time to go back to work again. Only once did he break and snap at me sarcastically, "Maybe the pixies did it."

Later that evening, William sneezed at that bit and asked,

"You don't think there was any truth in what he said?" The two of us were squeezed into my tiny above-shop apartment's dining nook. Over garlic cream pasta, I'd told him about my progress (or lack thereof).

"No, I don't," I told him, continuing to shove pasta in my face. Shock can take your appetite away, but I've found investigating gives it back double.

Across from me at the table, William rumbled. "You never know what they might be up to. Especially with the Meeting going on, and all those sorcerers in town."

"You just want the pixies to be on the hook for a murder," I retorted.

"Maybe." William shook floppy black ears, and sneezed. "They're dangerous. They say they just want light and sparkles and fun, but underneath it they'll turn you into a mulberry bush just for a lark. And no one ever says anything about it."

"A mulberry bush. Pretty specific. Personal experience?"

"You don't come back from spells like that, Red. The evidence is all around you. Have you ever wondered why the plants are so plentiful around here?"

"Because the environment is perfect for growing?"

"Because the pixies'll charm you out of your body as soon as your soul," growled William.

"Uh-huh. I do think we should go to them, though," I said conversationally as I poured myself a little more wine. More wine was always a good preparation for telling William something he didn't want to hear.

True to expectation, William's response shook the table. I deftly raised my glass as he shouted, the words coming out bark-like. "Why would you do that if you don't think they had anything to do with Finn? Are you *trying* to come up with stupid things to do?"

"No," I said calmly, sipping my wine. "I don't think they had anything to do with Finn. But they might have known about Qilin." There was a sharp-edged silence from William across the table, and I went on, "Come on, think about it. Qilin had been down there in that lake a long time, right? And no one's been here longer than the pixies. They founded the town, after all. And honestly with this whole carousel horse thing in general we've been avoiding them—"

"—for good reason," William interjected—

"—but they probably have valuable insight, given that all the horses seem to be converging around this 'Meeting' that they're holding!"

William glared at me with beady eyes for a very long moment. Then he huffed. "You're going, aren't you? Ugh. I'm coming too."

***

I don't want to make it sound like William always gets the last word in. Because he doesn't. Not if I can help it . . . but sometimes, I can't. I had *wanted* to take someone, really anyone, else. But Officer Thorn was busy with security for the festival; in her investigation, she'd run across a local thug who tipped her off to the fact that someone "wanted" something valuable in town. I guess, in thug-speak, that translates to "a theft is brewing." My other partner-in-preventing-crime, Luca, was busy with books.

"I can't get away right now," he'd hissed at me through a half-cracked door. He worked at the local bookshop, where apparently he was also imprisoned. "Owl is really in a mood lately."

"But the shop should be closed by now," I pointed out.

"We *are* closed. But after that thing with the miners, Owl's making me rearrange all the maps of town based on new criteria, and he's fussing about each step. *No one* knows this town like Owl. Do you *know* how hard it is to arrange a collection for someone who knows so much about the subject in question that they second-guess every tiny choice??"

"Okay, okay, I get it, you're not free," I said, throwing up my hands. The truth is, I *did* know what that was like, because William complained at me ferociously for being just as nit-picky whenever I needed help rearranging the chemicals in my lab.

And so, it was just me and said big black non-dog ambling through the festival as the sun set. It was one of the last nights of the pixies' month-long revel with sorcerers from all across Beyond, and in celebration of a happy Meeting—or maybe in celebration that the sorcerers would be leaving soon; I couldn't say—the pixies had opened up their home to mortals of all stripes in the evening for a banquet. Truthfully it had been William's plan to attend this in order to talk to some pixies, and a good one too, because my plan had been to rove the hillsides until anything remotely fey caught wind of me.

"All these colors and lights are giving me a headache," the familiar in question groused.

I looked around as we walked. The colors and lights William was complaining about were in fact the bright decorations of the Meeting stalls. Like a county fair, the Meeting sprawled across the fields outside of Belville, and to get to the pix-ies' banquet we were cutting right through the merchants' section of the festival. Whimsical and intricately-designed displays surrounded us: jars of dried things from miles—or perhaps ages—away, spinning racks of iridescent feathers, pots overflowing with ever-blooming flowers, heaps of sparkling mechanical marvels. I couldn't look at it all too carefully, because if I did, I wouldn't be able to resist the urge to stop and examine every little thing. Not only would we miss the pixies' banquet, I'd also miss opening my shop for about the next two years.

William made a point of stepping heavily on my boot, his upturned nose nudging against my hip. "Do I need to remind you, Red, not to eat anything they offer you?"

Distracted from staring, I took a deep breath. The air was thick with the smell of fried festival food and herby forest pies, the delectable scent of maple sugar the literal icing on top of the cake. "Why's there so much food around if no one can eat it?" I asked stubbornly.

"The sorcerers can if they have the proper protections up. *You* aren't a sorcerer, and I'm not about to battle a flying rat for your soul," William warned.

"Don't be rude," I reprimanded. "Especially since we're guests. Us and the rest of the town, it sounds like. That must be it up there," I said, spying ring upon ring of concentric fairy lights on the hilltop ahead. My steps picked up. William shoulder-checked some moon-eyed fair-goers out of the way to keep pace.

The evening light seemed suspended in the air, right above the golden glow of the dancing lights. They really were dancing, swaying in haphazard lines and circles all across the hillside, just above the visitors' heads. In this strange cacophony of light, everyone looked unearthly. I got to the edges of a crowd and hesitated. I saw many people I recognized—a neighbor of mine, Gloria, had her nose buried in some flowers not too far away, and jack-of-all-trades Dusty was stuffing his face full of cakes by a buffet table (perhaps gnomes were more resistant to fey magic? I had no idea). But I realized that even though the pixies had opened up their sacred home to visitors, I wasn't sure how to find a pixie to talk to.

What I was sure of, though, was that we were in the pixie's home. It's difficult to put into words: William has tried multiple times. As far as I remember, the gist is that pixie magic is illusion magic (except, I guess, when they're turning mortals into bushes). So, they can make a familiar road look unfamiliar to lead someone astray. Or, they can hide their home in plain sight. That's what they usually do—hide their headquarters; but for the banquet it was wide open, and I knew we were there because space and time were a little . . . woozy. It was like the entire world was rose-tinted and soft at the edges. Each person I looked at seemed completely new, even though I must have seen them around town.

I glanced down at William, relieved to find him still dark and shaggy and short-tempered.

"Cursed lights and dances and incessant music," he was mumbling as he sniffed the air.

His actions gave me an idea, and I nudged him with my knee. "Hey, can you smell them? The pixies?"

William's reply came with a disdainful sneeze. "How many times do I have to tell you people I'm not a real dog? I get it if Thorn can't remember, but you ought to know better."

"Ah, but you do such a convincing job of looking like one," I teased, grinning. I scanned the crowd again. Most people were milling around clumps of tables that resembled mushrooms; others were grouped under a long string of lights that seemed to delineate a game field of some kind. I was tempted to pull my alchemists' goggles over my eyes and see if they helped at all, when a shrill voice sounded at my elbow.

"Oooo! Good at costumes, is he? I want to see!"

The pixie was about a foot tall, bright orange cloaked in long tendrils of green with yellow wings. Its large dark eyes darted from me to William eagerly as it hovered in the air. *Of course* a pixie would show up not when we wanted it to, but when we had something intriguing to offer.

And of course, just as I was seeing how pixie-diplomacy might work, William had to go and ruin it. "It's not a costume," he snapped up at the creature, "and I don't do shows."

I rolled my eyes. *He has no trouble lying about* me *when it suits him. Why can't he lie to keep a pixie's attention for a while?* "You know what he's *really* good at," I said hastily, before the pixie lost interest, "is making things sparkle and glow."

"Eh," said the pixie, wavering. "We do that all the time."

"Thank the gods," William huffed. He nudged me rather than use my name. "Ask your questions and be done with it!"

"Oooo!" The pixie's eyes lit with interest once more. "You have *questions?* Then I have answers!"

"You do? Great. You see—"

"Of course I do, silly," the pixie continued. "Because that's how the game works!"

"Um, no, I was hoping —"

In an instant, the world shifted. I had exactly zero chance to explain to the pixie that I'd actually hoped this would be a serious interview rather than a *game.* You know, something full of weight and respect for the dead? Instead, I found myself catching my breath in a very different world.

It was lighter—much lighter. I was still standing on grass, but the plants themselves were lit up like they were coated in glow-powder. There were patches of all different colors: pink, blue, green, yellow, all spread out around me. I couldn't see the pixie any more, but I was conscious of its attention—or maybe the attention of a crowd. There definitely was a boundary that surrounded us.

Us . . .

"William?!" I cried out, trying to look around and see anything other than glowy grass and dark sky.

"Red, you need to—oof—*move!*"

William's voice came from far away. I was puzzled, because he'd been right next to me before. But as the mists cleared a bit more I could see that he was on the other side of the hill, leaping through patches of color. *But why move?*

The reason became clear when beneath me the yellow-colored grass upended itself and I was dumped head over heels, falling, clutching at a ledge of earth and finally scrambling onto a red patch nearby.

"Get—to—the middle!" William bayed.

And *that's* when I understood. I was a sweaty, dirt-covered game piece. William and I both were. And the hillside had become a giant game board.

"That's it!" the pixie's voice fell from the sky, laced with delight. "If you want answers you have to find common ground. Got to keep up! Go on, go on!"

I leapt up to my feet, ready to get my bearings properly this time. The patches of color were laid out regularly—not in any pattern that I could see, but all of the same size. They glowed and pulsed and then, as I had just experienced, they flipped.

"And William thinks the way out of this is to get to the middle," I muttered, scanning. Between William's dark fluffy shape and me, there was a violet square, probably halfway up the hill. "Well, times like these, William knows bes—"

A sudden pulse all around my ankles reminded me that I didn't have time to think. Maybe that's what I don't like about games: not having the time to consider each choice. There's always social pressure and sometimes even timers and, occasionally, huge flip-flopping slabs of topsoil that want to interrupt your thoughts.

The pixie's voice again rang over our heads. "Why would we want your souls when they make you such *excellent* players?"

I dodged to a green pad as fast as I could, then to a blue one. Another yellow to my left flipped, and the red in front of me pulsed. That, I was sure, was the warning signal. But where else could I go? I had to keep moving, like William said. I looked over and saw that he, too, was on a pulsing red pad. *Here's for solidarity,* I thought, and threw myself forward.

I didn't *mean* to get walloped by the overturning square again; I had every intention of hopping on to the next green square beyond the red one. But my foot slipped as I hit the red grass, and I went tumbling down. I caught my breath and did my best to brace myself for the flip—

But it didn't come.

Curious, I popped my head up to see where William had gone. He was still on his red pad, too.

"Hey," I cried out to the watching pixie—or pixies—"you didn't mention the rules!"

"Rules? No one likes rules!" the pixie laughed.

Around me, the pad had stopped pulsing. I looked around, pursing my lips. *I* like rules.

Across the hill, William growled and leapt from his pad. "Come on, Red, stop musing!"

Immediately, mine flipped and my stomach plummeted and I got a healthy mouthful of dirt as I struggled into the safety of a green square.

"William," I cried back, spitting out dirt, "what if we don't have to get to the middle? What if we just have to stay on the same color?"

"What?" William skidded to a halt on a blue square, his ears flopping, shedding blades of grass.

"We were just on the same color and it didn't—" I paused to dodge onto a yellow—"flip!"

"Yeah, but the game also didn't *end*," William said, jumping onto a yellow pad himself and baring his teeth like he'd prefer to take a bite out of the flipping pad behind him.

"Maybe it would have if we'd stayed there longer!"

"No way. They're going to have us doing circles all night!"

"I don't know," I said reasonably, "we seem okay right—"

A chorus of pixies laughed as the pad under me flipped and I dove for blue.

"Not the color," William called out helpfully. "The symbol, Red! Look at the symbols!"

I struggled to get up this time. My shoulder had taken a direct hit, and my leggings were too thin for this rolling-around-in-the-grass nonsense. *What symbols?* I wondered, shaking my head. Another peal of laughter from the unseen pixies reminded me to keep moving.

Above me, there was nothing. And there was nothing on the field except me and William, who was currently hopping in a wide circuit around the field as pads between him and the center continuously flipped. But William had said he'd seen symbols . . . hopefully he hadn't made that up. I dodged onto a green square and stared hard at the ground. It was the only other place a symbol could be.

There was . . . something. Really it could have just been overturned dirt. There was plenty of *that* to go around. William howled something unintelligible at me and I dodged again. This time when I stared at the ground, I pulled my goggles over my face.

And the sight of a dog hit my eyes so brightly from among the grasses that I stumbled backward into an overturning square.

"What the—"

"There's butterflies," William called. "And birds."

What? I pried a tiny rock out of my front teeth and threw it away, and William's words clicked. "There's dogs!" I yelled back.

"Of course there is," William huffed as he ran by on my right. "Because they think they're bloody *funny!*"

I ignored his spite—which honestly, I was starting to share—and rolled to the next square. "This one has a fish."

"I'm not running any more," William declared flatly from the far side of the field. "This one has a horse. A red horse. Find one of those!"

"Aww, he rooted himself to the spot," said a pixie voice.

"Oo, should we help?" asked another.

Taking from their insight that William was serious and the danger had not passed, I began looking hurriedly. In the grass to my left I caught sight of a horse's flared tail—but it was blue. "Does this work?" I hopped on to it, and immediately drew the pixies' amusement to myself as my pad flipped.

"Okay, no go," I said, leaping before their damn dirt-clod could catch me. Amid sighs of disappointment, I spotted a flowing mane—a red one. I ran for it, but the yellow square between me and it pulsed. With each step it pulsed brighter.

"I *refuse* to be intimidated," I panted to the ground. I launched myself into the air.

And landed with a hard thud right on the back of a red, prancing horse.

The pixies erupted. "They got it!"

I got to my feet, pushing my goggles up wearily. The sky seemed to be raining confetti. It had returned to its twilight glow: once more, light was coming from above, not below. The hillside had been returned to normal, except for the red outline of a carousel horse beneath my feet.

And William's. He was right back at my side, and snarling. "I *told* you."

"The horse has the answer!" The pixie literally danced before our eyes. I looked around, wary, but there was no one else to be seen.

"You mean Qilin? Or the one that talks?" asked William, naming carousel horses we'd already collected. Each of the little statues was connected to a myth, and came with a unique spell.

"Neither," the pixie replied with glee. "It's *this* one, silly!"

Immediately a horse materialized behind the pixie. It *was* a carousel horse, like the ones we'd gathered throughout Belville, but unlike my growing collection of statuettes, this one was full-sized. It was much more stately than the others, too; there was an ancient air to it, and it looked like it had been carved out of pure limestone. Its neck curved, muscles bulged. The look in its dark stone eyes was so dignified that for a moment I forgot we were dealing with anything as ridiculous as game-playing pixies.

"Right," said William, glowing beside me. "And this one's power is . . ."

The pixie fluttered down to William's height and delicately bopped his nose. "It *has* a name," the pixie pointed out. "You have to be very respectful. It's called Astarte."

William whined. "Red, I don't think we want this one."

"I didn't want any of them," I whispered back. Louder, I said, "Look, all I want to know is if you know who killed Finn. And—everyone else. If you do know, I want to know who the murderer is. And, I guess, anything you know about the carousel horses, since apparently you have one."

"That's three questions," the pixie pointed out. "A good number!" It twirled up through the air. "But not really good questions," it added, pausing as though the thought had just struck it. "Because you already know the answers to all of them."

I sidled. Was that carousel horse's eye glinting at me? "What do you mean?"

"You *must* already know," the pixie continued. "And that's why we brought out Astarte. She's much too serious for us, you know. But we got her from a sorcerer at the very first Meeting and he said only to give her away to someone with a good cause! And finding who killed those poor people is a good cause, we all agreed. Plus *someone* has to look after the horses, because the bad people are getting too close. So you can have her . . . *if* you can say who killed them."

I gnashed my teeth, looking at the horse again. "But that's why I came *here*—"

"Red," William hissed, leaning into my thigh. "Don't push your luck. That thing means business."

I got the feeling he wasn't talking about the pixie. I had never heard the word *Astarte*, but from William's agitation, it was reasonable to suppose that it was associated with powerful myth.

Power makes fools reckless and sages careful, my mother had always said. I crossed my arms and considered my questions again:

One: do the pixies know who killed Finn and Kit. Well, I reasoned, obviously, they do. But they must not care enough to do something about it. Or they've been too busy with their Meeting. Who knows?

Two: who was it. The pixie says I already know. Okay, we'll come back to that in a minute.

Three: do they know about the carousel horses: clearly, yes. But only because of some sorcerer however long ago. Maybe, like William, they don't want to mess with whatever power the horses have.

I blew out a breath, puffing strands of long hair out of my face.

"Come on," said the pixie, flying in a careful circle around the limestone horse and hovering above—not touching—the golden pole at its center. "The murderer needs to be stopped. Pixies don't do that kind of thing, but you can. But Astarte can help you! You just have to say who it is first."

"Fine." Mentally, I ran through Thorn's list of suspects. It wasn't long. Knee was out, as far as I could tell. My heart ached as I thought of the poor boy. The sorcerers and the pixies, who might be interested in the carousel horses, didn't seem too interested in Finn—or in keeping Astarte, so why would they murder someone for another horse? Lark, local mine owner, hadn't shown any interest in Lake Lava or its contents; as a newcomer, she could even be expected to know that Qilin was down there waiting to murder trespassers. She was more bothered with digging railroad tunnels.

I was still thinking of Lark and her tunnels when a shock ran through me. *Owl's making me rearrange all the maps after that thing with the miners,* Luca had said. The thing with the miners, which had happened very shortly before Finn's intrusion into the lake and his subsequent death. *No one knows this town like Owl.*

Oh no, I thought. William whined beside me again, calling my attention to the fact that I'd begun tapping my foot rapidly. *Thorn said a thug she picked up told her someone in town's looking for things. And someone who'd know there was anything worth looking for in the first place would be . . . Owl.*

"Aha!" the pixie crowed again, reading my face. "She has it! She has it!"

"Do you?" William jerked his head up at me.

I ran my hand through my hair, knocking my goggles askew. "It's—it could be—I think," I admitted, sighing, "It's Owl."

There was a brightness all around us, like we were inside one of the pixies' sparkling lights. The voices of the pixies faded into the voices of the crowd. With a feeling of coming back down to earth, William and I were at the banquet once more.

"No one wants to talk about murder," the pixie informed us, wavering. Just before it flew off, it added, "Thanks for the game!"

"Thanks for the . . . horse," I said, a bit forlornly, looking down at the carousel horse in my hand. It was a tiny version of the one the pixie had called Astarte. Even when pocket-sized, it looked every bit as serious as the pixies weren't.

"Well," huffed William, "the pixies certainly think you're

right. But you better have more proof than that before you go blighting a respected local scholar."

"Is that what it does?" I asked, still staring at the horse, oblivious to the cheerful company all around us.

William shook his floppy ears, his fur glowing blue as he used his magic to scan the carousel horse. "Might be able to make things grow, too. Seems like the spell on it has a few layers. It's not surprising . . . Astarte was many things to many people. The horse was only one of her symbols."

"Okay, so she was a goddess, then? Of what, justice?" I figured that'd make sense, given the situation in which we'd been given her. "Please don't say games."

"Nope." William huffed again. "Fertility, love, harvests—and war."

* * *

When William and I finally caught up with Officer Thorn and shared our findings, at first she just stared at the horse in my hand.

Then she stood. "Nothing for it," she declared, "but to go and ask some questions. Come along! Hup hup!"

With identical helpless looks, William and I fell in behind her. But when we got to the bookstore . . .

There was no one there. No Owl. No Luca.

"Really?" William cocked his head as Thorn rattled doors and rifled through drawers. The shop hadn't even been locked. "I thought they pretty much live here."

"They do," Officer Thorn confirmed. "There's two apartments above this floor. But something must have tipped them off."

"You're talking like Owl's definitely guilty," I pointed out. "That's an assumption at this point."

"Says the woman holding a magical horse of punishment," Thorn retorted. "Like a nightmare. Ha, get it? Okay, we're going to need a surveillance spell on this place, stat. I'll talk to the Guild—"

"Wait," I interjected. "You're also talking like Luca was in on it too."

"Well, he isn't here," William observed dryly.

"But he could just as easily be in danger!"

Officer Thorn gave me an almost pitying look. "You go on home, Red. You got a good lead here. It's my move now."

I didn't necessarily want to agree, but I also didn't want to stay. I followed William as he traced his way through town back to my shop. It's a good thing he was there, because I wasn't thinking about routes or potions. Instead, I kept replaying that conversation with the pixie back over in my mind.

And you know, I think that's what I *really* hate about games. It's not the frivolity or the time limits. It's that, in order to win—to get something right—you often have to give something up.

I clutched the carousel horse Astarte in my hand. Maybe, as goddess of love and war, she knew exactly what I meant.

9

A Silver Churning

The Ninth Carousel Caper

How do you catch a criminal?

The same way you'd catch anyone: offer up something they want.

Such, I gathered, was Officer Thorn's thinking. And as the lone half-orc policewoman in charge of keeping the peace in small-town Belville, she'd apparently given this a lot of thought.

"Red," said she, having burst into my potions shop right at closing time. It was an improvement: at least she hadn't come over right when the thought struck her, because not even a sorcerer could have caught my attention during the afternoon rush of fair-going shoppers. The pixies' Meeting festival was due to end on the next day, and that couldn't come soon enough. "Red. I've decided."

"Great," I replied blearily, watching the officer throw herself into the armchair reserved for patrons waiting for custom orders. I was holding my cleaning bottle and a balled-up apron, and struggling to remember my own name. Good thing she said it twice. "Decided about what, exactly?"

"Those horses. The murders—all of them. Owl. It's one and the same," said Thorn. "He's been behind this all along, hiring thugs, hiring Beth, attacking Kit. Don't you see?"

I swayed on sore feet, thinking. The very first time I'd encountered trouble, when someone had tried to steal the first carousel horse, the thief had mentioned a 'Grand Sorcerer.' Owl was not a sorcerer of any quality, as far as I knew. *But the whole thing* could *have been a cover,* I realized. *Maybe he contracted the thieves while pretending to be a sorcerer, because no one would question another powerful mage in town for the Meeting . . . but why go to all the trouble?* Word was that when all the carousel horses were gathered together, they were powerful enough to destroy the world; perhaps that in itself answered my question.

"Done counting the money," called William, my magical canine-shaped companion. He popped his head over the sales counter and looked between me and Thorn. "You aren't trying to talk to Red, are you?" he asked her. "She sold enough potions today to buy a trip to Never Never Land *and* some custom enchanted glass shoes. Probably used up all the brain cells she had left."

"I did not," I protested.

"Think about it," insisted Thorn, taking no notice of either of us. "He sent Finn to his death in search of that horse—Qilin. That's one. But who's to say he hasn't been searching for all of them, all along? There was that robbery at Cairn's antiques, where Beth had been told to send the white horse to someone—someone we never did find. Someone who murdered Kit on the road. What if Lark was only interested in the things to sell them? Who, then, was buying? It was Owl!"

"But Owl was invited to the party where we found the second horse, the storm horse," I recalled uncertainly. "And everyone who'd been invited turned out to be very helpful. I don't think they would have included Owl on the guestlist if he was out to get all the horses and everyone near them."

Officer Thorn responded by pointing at me with such excitement that I startled. "Keep your friends close and your enemies closer. He might've revealed himself if he was there. Instead, he sent Luca, and used information from him to figure out where the other horses were!"

Luca. The bookstore clerk had disappeared when Owl had, two days ago. William thought the two were in cahoots, and apparently Thorn might too, but I had a terrible feeling in my stomach that said maybe they weren't. Maybe Luca needed our help.

"Alright, fine," I said to Officer Thorn. "If you're right about Owl, then what do you propose we do next?"

* * *

"This," said William, quite definitely, "sucks."

"Shut up," I hissed back. "It'll be worth it. It's *got* to be."

We stood side by side behind a fair table, dressed in identical gingham aprons. *It's my best idea ever,* Thorn had said. *There's no way he'll be able to resist,* she had said.

We were also huddled under our bright purple awning,

because it was *pouring* rain.

"Hi," I said as brightly as I could to yet another curious, umbrella-toting fairgoer, while William simply growled. "Care to play our guessing game?"

Officer Thorn knew quite well that William and I had to play a "game" with the pixies to get our most recent horse, a representation of the goddess Astarte. *That's what gave me the idea,* she'd beamed. Meanwhile my legs were sore and I could still taste dirt from the playing field. Games would *not* have been my go-to solution for luring in a murderer.

To be fair to Thorn, though, the idea was solid: offer up carousel-horse-Astarte as bait to catch the attention of a carousel-horse-mad criminal. In her search of Owl's bookstore, she'd stumbled across an old scroll about Astarte which went on and on for *yards* about the goddess's many powers and myths. And, promptly, she'd confiscated it. So that was the game: guess how long the scroll actually was, and you could win a horse statuette.

At first, I thought the whole thing was ridiculously simple. And now that I was in the early stages of an evening packed with one sticky-sweet fairgoer after another, I could tell it was going to be a hard slog. But Thorn had spent a full day putting up flyers and spreading the word about our game—and particularly its prize—and she was *positive* that on this day, the last day of the Meeting, she was going to catch Owl as he attempted to steal our carousel horse.

And if we caught Owl, I reminded myself, we should be able to find Luca.

So I put back my shoulders and gave a charmed ticket to a little gnome-child in a poncho several sizes too big, so that she could write down her guess in hopes of winning the "horsey."

An elf couple, our old friend Ryuko, a gaggle of blue- and green-skinned teens who seemed to be loving the rain, and an elderly woman who had to be at *least* half fairy followed. All their tickets went into our collections jar, which was now about a quarter full.

William looked on glumly. "The evening's barely begun," he pointed out. "You might need a bigger jar."

"Then you can magic this one bigger," I retorted. I wasn't really certain that was something he could do, but I'd had enough of his moping. Working this fair needed to be a team effort—or at least not a twenty-mile race with an anchor strapped to my back.

"Or just throw the tickets away," Thorn suggested brightly from my left. I turned to find her lurking outside our hastily-erected stall, pressing under the edge of our shelter. She had mud halfway up her legs and hands full of fried vegetables wrapped in colorful napkins.

"Don't say that so loudly," I said, watching as a troll and a human broke from the throng and sauntered to our table.

"Why not? The posters only say you *could* win a horse," Thorn informed me. A large floret of battered cauliflower disappeared, and she licked her fingers. "Not that anyone will."

"Taking this really seriously, are you?" William huffed. I nudged him towards our newest customers. Thorn might have come up with a guessing game, but between her and William, the preferred game was bickering.

As William reluctantly explained the game to the grinning couple, I said quietly to Thorn, "Do you really think this will work?"

"Of course I do," said she, pouring golden-coated snap peas

into her mouth. Over the munching, she continued, "What, you want me to tell you 'no,' when you're already here and in uniform? Ha! Listen," she added more seriously, swallowing, "the festival's only beginning. Dances and demonstrations'll start soon, and music, and when it gets proper dark is when they'll do fireworks and the whole bit. I'd bet my last coin that during one of those distractions, our target'll show."

"In this weather?"

"A little rain never hurt anybody," Thorn informed me.

"It's just, we *have* bet our last coin. Last carousel horse, that is." I glanced behind my shoulder, where—displayed proudly on a shelf—the little horse Astarte sat. Thorn had insisted we have it there, even if we didn't give it away, and for once William had agreed. Someone had been trying to scry on us for days, he'd said, and that someone was most likely Owl. Scrying was a magical form of spying which William, as a familiar particularly strong in protective magics, could sense and deflect. At least, he could if he or I was the target; not if Thorn was. And so, he decided, it was best that she be as authentic as possible. The mystery scrier wouldn't be able to read her thoughts or hear her words, but they might be able to see her actions.

Thorn paused halfway through a "blooming" onion, looking at me askance. "Worried, Red?"

"Not about the horse exactly. Just about—" I waved a hand, and sighed. "What might happen."

I'm an alchemist by trade. *All* the magic carousel horses, with their strange and powerful charms, make me nervous. Even the useful ones—those which granted the user speed, or could give advice. And the thing is, Astarte's power wasn't only useful: it was *frightening*. William's insights about it had been along the lines of "blight" and "war." To me, the whole carousel horse venture felt like playing with fire—something I only do in laboratory conditions, when other people aren't around, and the most that might get blown up is my eyebrows.

"I'm going to be right here all evening," Thorn reminded me, finishing off her "salad." "I'll be on him like green on plants. Ha. Get it?"

I frowned at her, but a twiglike person under a huge parasol chose that moment to distract me. As I explained the game once more—I had it down pat by now—I became aware of another sound over my own voice.

Shouts. And they weren't shouts of "encore" or "brava," either.

Thorn was gone before I turned around. She didn't need me saying, "hey, are you sure you don't have to go check that out?" to do her job. But as I helped the next three, five, then ten customers, the hairs on the back of my neck stood up. I started to get restless.

"Stop doing that thing with your feet," William complained. "You're stirring up the puddle under the table and it's splashing me. Oh, hello, fine, yes, you can guess how long the scroll is . . ."

". . . . thank you, we'll be in touch if you're right, enjoy the festival," I finished, then muttered as another customer walked away, "I'm *not* doing anything with my feet. Did you hear that?"

"The thing that was probably just a distraction to lure Thorn and all the other guards away from us? Yeah. No, we won't unroll the scroll first so you can measure it," William barked to a curious heckler.

Of course he'd see it that way, I told myself. The thing was, it was kind of nice to hear someone else voice the fears in my head aloud. Nice—and morbid. I handed a ticket to my friend and on-call maintenance gnome Dusty completely on autopilot as my mind continued to race and my feet, left unattended, continued pacing in place.

"*Red,*" William grumbled, as another group of neighbors approached and I still wasn't, well, still.

"I can't believe you didn't tell me about this," said a dark-robed figure, coming to rest on the other side of the table. A hood obscured most of its head, but the words were light and friendly.

"Luca," I said automatically. My feet rooted themselves to the ground. I stared at him open-mouthed. "Luca, where have you been?"

"I'll tell you all about it later," he promised, his green eyes on mine. "When we're somewhere less crowded, okay? Right now, I have a carousel horse to win. After all the reading I've done for the other horses, this should be a cinch!"

I watched as he actually rubbed his hands together and grinned. Next to me, William whined. I had to admit it *was* like Luca to focus on a competition when more important matters were at hand . . . and yet, how could he have gotten away from Owl? What if he'd been put up to this?

And then he looked at me again, green eyes alight. And my fears took a darker turn. *What if that isn't Luca at all? What if it's someone else using glamour magic?*

After all, if Owl was willing to impersonate a sorcerer, why not a clerk?

"Come on." He continued grinning at me. Dark skin, black robe, all blended into the gloom of the rain—except his eyes. "You know I'll just give it back to you if I win. This is a matter of scholarly principle. *No one* knows scrolls better than me! Let's see, can I ask questions? Does this one cover Astarte's role as fertility goddess as well as the stories of her in battle?"

"That's a William question," I muttered, nudging my companion forward so I could keep thinking.

The thing is, it's really easy to look like something else. It's so easy that it's become a platitude. *Appearances can be deceiving.* You don't have to be a sorcerer or a witch to buy yourself a glamour spell and look like someone different—I sell things in my very own shop that can alter appearances. However, everything I sell is temporary, and the effects never cover fingerprints or the soles of the feet, to comply with the law in Pastoria. Not to mention my own moral code.

If you want to pass yourself off as someone else, the real trick is getting their mannerisms right.

". . . really fascinating," Luca was saying to William. "And you're sure the horse is a symbol of her? Not one of the other ancient deities?"

William bristled. "Given that the thing shares her name, I think anyone might be able to figure it out."

"Right, right, and your feelings about these have been good so far," said Luca soothingly. He looked thoughtfully, intently, up at the carousel horse behind us.

"Go on then, fill out a ticket," I decided, passing a slip to him. William looked up at me as Luca reached for it. Beneath the table, I tapped my toes twice. It was a secret signal between us from our days on the road. It meant *no.*

Just as Luca leaned on the table, scrawling out his answer with a scholar's horrible penmanship, Officer Thorn emerged from the crowd on her way back to us. She was talking before she reached the booth, saying loudly,

"It's a Finn situation, Red—"

Finn. Murder and theft. Carousel horses.

"—keep your eyes open, our guest is around somewhere!"

"I know," I returned calmly, watching the hood of Luca's robe as he bent over the paper. "He's right here."

He must have been waiting for me to say that: maybe he knew I was on to him. Maybe he knew, deep down, that by questioning William he'd given himself away. Maybe Thorn came back quicker than he expected, and he realized he had to be ready to run. Or maybe this was part of his plan all along. Owl, still in his guise as Luca, shot up over the table and grabbed the carousel horse behind me before turning on his heel and sprinting into the crowd.

"Oh no you don't!!"

William was after him in a moment, and they were two black blurs against the many-colored festival crowd. In a landscape like a drowned watercolor, they were heavy blots. Standers-by and lookers-on fell to both sides as Owl streaked through the festival tents. William followed in leaps and bounds. With each long stride, William glowed brighter and brighter, his dark fur tinged in blue light—a sign of his powers as a familiar. He wasn't going to let Owl get away.

There was a brief instant, right then. Right when William made his final leap. Thorn and I were in pursuit, following the path of destruction, and I could see it clearly. Owl turned and looked over his shoulder, and saw William coming. And he clutched a knife in his hand. In the rain and fairy lights, it glinted.

And that's when I realized that to catch a thief, you can't just offer up something they want. You also have to be willing to lose everything else. Because *they* are. They have nothing to lose.

"Nooooooo!"

I cried out a second before it happened, I think. My voice seemed to surprise everyone around me. And that was for the best—because however fast William and Owl had been going, I tripled, even quadrupled that speed. I barreled after them both and hurled myself at them, hands outstretched. But even though I'd called out an instant before it happened, I got there an instant too late. William had already collided with Owl's knife by the time I collided with them both.

The three of us hit the ground hard and I was *furious.* I yanked Owl away from William and pinned him to the ground, tearing at him, screaming at him. I'm not even sure what I was saying. But I know what I was thinking: *I have to save William.*

And in my passion my hand knocked into a carousel horse. Not Astarte—Owl was clutching that desperately with his other hand. Instead, from the inside of his sleeve, I'd knocked free a different horse. A new one.

The one Thorn was talking about when she said "Finn." There must have been another horse at the festival, and Owl murdered its owner to get it before he came to us.

This realization came afterward, though. All I knew in the moment was that suddenly I was drenched, and not because of the rain. As the little horse clattered to the ground, wave upon wave of a milk-white ocean sprang from it, covering Owl and me and everyone around us. Covering William.

Owl sputtered and protested, saying something about an "Elixir of Life" and "you've ruined everything." *Typical criminal talk,* I decided dismissively. Finally distracted from my anger, I turned away from him—probably kicking him for good measure—and scooted through the strange, glittering water to get to William.

He had been motionless. My un-familiar, my companion, my friend. He had been lying there on his side with no sound and no magic, but as the waves surged around him, he lifted his head. He saw me looking at him with five different kinds of panic written across my face, and he snorted.

"Red," he asked, "are you going to tell me you haven't even heard of the King of Horses?"

* * *

Uchaishravas. That, I soon learned, was the name of the King of Horses. He came from Hindu myth, and he was associated with not only milky seas but the Elixir of Life.

That was the only information which would stick in my over-worked brain, however: the finer points of William's self-important lecture about the importance of Uchaishravas were lost on me, because I was too busy hugging the snot out of him. And then shouting a bit at Owl. And then helping Thorn clean the whole scene up. And, finally, *finally,* taking a warm shower back at home and settling onto my tiny sofa wrapped in a comfy, fluffy robe.

The lights of the festival were barely visible through my apartment's windows, a fuzzy anomaly against the stormy summer night sky. All of the noise of the festival, thankfully, was locked outside. William stretched out on the rug in front of me, munching tea leaves (familiars have strange ideas about what counts as "food") which smelled very strongly of peppermint.

"I suppose," I mused aloud, letting my head fall back on the sofa's arm, "it's a better smell than wet dog."

William's jaws smacked. "I never smell. I don't really have a true body. So I can't be smelly, and I also can't be *dead*."

"You keep saying that, but you certainly looked the part. Maybe Owl's knife was enchanted or something."

"Maybe you're crazy."

"Maybe you're unnerved," I pointed out. "Which is fine. I know *I* was."

"I was just dazed by you knocking us all over, and that silly charm on the carousel horse woke me up," William insisted. Waves of peppermint washed over me as he huffed.

"Whatever," said I, conceding the point. "I'm just glad things turned out the way they did." And I was—I really, really was. Sitting there, warm, quiet, surrounded by the smells of tea, I was struck by a sense of deep appreciation and contentment. There was only one thing still bothering me.

"That's the last of the horses," William was saying, "if the Talking Horse and its riddles were right. Which they were, if I had to bet. Nine is an important number when it comes to groups of things, you know. Three by three, as the sorcerers say—"

"Please, goddess, no more sorcerers," I interrupted. I was glad to hear that William thought our carousel horse troubles were over—and they must be, I figured, since Owl was safely locked up in Thorn's police station. But that hadn't been what was on my mind. "The *real* problem is that we still don't know where Luca is."

"The problem, Red, is that all the horses together are—"

"—I know they're supposed to be dangerous, but they haven't done anything yet. Your wards are doing just fine and in the meantime we *still* haven't found him!"

"— are a target, I was going to say. Red, you can't worry so much about the rest of it. Thorn will get it out of Owl eventually," said William with rare faith in our local officer.

And even rarer, his faith was misplaced. I hate to say it, but the truth is, William is usually right about a lot of things. And Officer Thorn is good at a lot of things, including catching criminals and figuring out their secrets. But when she came by the next afternoon to check on us—we'd slept right through the morning—she brought no encouraging news.

"He insists no harm has come to the boy," Thorn reported from the doorway, "but he says, and I quote, 'not even you could find him where he's gone.' I think he means *you*, Red. Does that mean anything to you?"

I shifted on my slippered feet. William gave me a look, but kept his mouth shut for once.

To catch a criminal, you have to give them something they want—even if only temporarily. So to find a friend, maybe you have to give up something you wanted to keep. A secret.

"It might," I admitted. "I don't know how Owl would know. But I am . . . I mean, I come from a tribe of Seers. Before all the—alchemy."

Officer Thorn whistled. "That was true? So you're a scientist *and* a Seer? How does that work, then? I always knew you'd make a good unofficial partner. Consider yourself on this case for *real*. Did you See any of this coming? Can you tell the future?"

"This is exactly why I don't tell people," I returned, sighing as she grinned widely. "And honestly I'm not any good at it. I never have been."

"'Strue," said William helpfully. "She couldn't have even guessed the length of the scroll at the fair."

"Maybe that's why the horses come to her, though." Thorn addressed William with a scholarly air. I realized that my admission was quickly getting out of hand.

"Eh, that could just be luck," William theorized. "Owl's right if he's talking about scrying or searching—"

"In this case, Owl is wrong," I interrupted firmly. I looked from one friend to another, more determined than ever to bring this crazy mess to a clean conclusion. "One way or another, we are going to find Luca. You can count on that. And then all this carousel horse nonsense will be at an end."

10

A Singing Epiphany

The Tenth Carousel Caper

"*Not even you could find him where he's gone.*"

That's what Owl, thief and murderer, had to say to me. He remained smug behind his prison bars, clearly enjoying the fact that even though we'd won the battle in bringing him in, we didn't have all the pieces. We couldn't find our friend Luca, the bookstore clerk. According to Owl, criminal mastermind and Luca's former employer, we never would.

It was a declaration of war, and it was pointed directly at *me*. Owl knew that, as the town's resident alchemist and "unofficial" police assistant, I'd been behind most of the carousel horse capers. He also knew that my dark skin and glittery hair weren't cosmetic: they betrayed my heritage—the fact that I came from a line of Seers. Normally I didn't

170

tell anyone that fact—I may have even lied to *obscure* that fact, if I'm honest—because I didn't like the explanations and expectations involved. But Owl must have thought that made it especially funny that I knew nothing about where Luca had gone.

I thought it was about time I pulled out all the stops.

And that's why I sat on my living room floor with my dog-shaped familiar William. The dining room table was overflowing with truesight vials, predicting potions, scrying bowls, and all other kinds of mumbo-jumbo which I as a scientist usually avoid. The coffee table was full of my more usual arsenal: Exploding Powder, Evaporating Powder, Faithful Acid (guaranteed to only melt what you want it to!), and slime (it had been useful once before, and we needed all the help we could get). The sofa was in total disarray and in fact invisible under a pile of maps of Belville. And on the rug before us was one dark carousel horse.

"This is it, this is it, this has got to be it," I muttered to myself, wiping my palms on my breeches. I sat hunched over, my foot already fallen asleep as I stared down the horse. The Talking Horse of Russian fairy tale.

"The *caballo marino* wasn't helpful," William reminded me. "Don't get your hopes up too far, Red."

"That was a *good* thing. The caballo-whatever sees ghosts. So, if it can't find him, we know he's alive."

"You know it isn't as easy as—"

"Not now," I interrupted without looking over my shoulder at William. To the horse, I said, "I want to know how to find Luca."

I faltered a little—just a little—at the end. I wasn't sure how much information the Talking Horse would need, and

I realized that I didn't actually *know* a whole lot about Luca. That is, I didn't know if he had any extra names or where he came from; that had never come up. I knew that he was loyal and enthusiastic and helpful and caring, but I wasn't sure that'd help find him.

The dark little carousel horse spoke as it had always spoken: deeply, and creepily, and without any hesitation. Answering my formatted question with a formulaic response of its own, it said,

"You will find the one you seek behind forgotten castle's keep. You must tread carefully in those halls, lest you trip and lose it all."

"Poetry. What is it with spells and poetry?" I sat back, my mind racing through how many castles might be in Belville.

"Do you really want me to explain that?" William huffed when I didn't respond. He poked the dark horse with one paw. "Is that all the cryptic non-help you needed? Because I'm going to put it back in its box if so. I don't like having any of them out for long, given how they're supposedly dangerous when they're all together—"

"Wait," I interrupted. "Remember way back in the spring, when we rescued Dusty from the druids in the forest? Wasn't *that* in an ancient castle?"

"Sure, feel free to carry on your own conversation and ignore my qu—"

"I think so too," I said, not totally registering that he hadn't said "sure" in agreement with me. "I think that's it. I have—I have a feeling about it."

William paused in his disapproval of my conduct, his shaggy black face and beady eyes appraising me coolly. "And when Red the Kicked-Out Seer has a 'good feeling,' we take that seriously?"

"Hey! I wasn't kicked out." I threw a pillow at him, unearthing it from a shower of maps. But the truth was, he had a point. Among my family my Seer instincts were famously lacking, and a 'good' sign to me might well be a warning. "I just know this is right, William. I—can't explain it. We need to go look, at least."

"Can't explain it, huh? That's how actual Seer stuff works." He looked at me a minute longer with his head cocked and his ears looking adorably—and annoyingly—fluffy. Then he sneezed. "All right, we'll go. In the morning. You do realize that it's past midnight now, right?"

* * *

"This," William growled, "does *not* count as morning."

I'd managed to get my night-owl companion out of bed, loaded up with friend-rescuing supplies and all the way to the abandoned castle in the woods before he thought to lodge this complaint.

"Please. The sun has completely risen. Officer Thorn was up. She thought it was very commendable for us to be out this early," I reminded him, since he probably didn't remember swinging by (stumbling by, in his case) the police station earlier that morning.

William groaned and plopped down onto the castle's front stoop. I had paused there myself, rummaging through the multitude of useful, magically-reinforced pockets hidden upon my person. When I'd decided to pull out the stops, I'd not been messing around. In addition to my usual arsenal, I was carrying seven charmed carousel horses. William, under protest, was carrying the other two. He insisted it was dangerous, because if one person ended up with all the horses, they might fall prey to some mysterious power or bloodthirsty thief. I insisted we needed all the help we could get. William insisted I was mental, and then I'd shoved him out the door.

"I promised Thorn I'd do this," I muttered, extricating a carved white horse from a flap somewhere down my thigh. The Wind Horse. When I held in my hands and activated the charm it carried, ghosts went flying out from its carousel pole and back in the direction of town—a signal to the officer that we'd arrived at the castle. With any luck, she and Ryuko and Cairn, the others who knew about the carousel horses, were already on their way to the castle as backup—but I hadn't wanted to wait, so William and I had gone on ahead.

"That was kinda neat," I said to William, rocking back on my heel from the ghostly force and tucking the horse away once more. "I never actually used that one before."

"I still don't see why you think we'll need to use any of them. You could have used Bottled Messenger—"

"—which we are out of, so it would have taken days to make, and as for the other horses, you never know what might happen. Besides, it's about time these things earned their keep."

"Uh-huh." William sat sniffing at the morning air. It was a bit chilly for a bright summer morning—or so it felt to me; but that might have been the castle. Tucked away in the forest, the strange, overgrown architectural monstrosity seemed to have its own time as well as its own weather. It was harmless—abandoned, supposedly. But the walls surrounding its four towers and the overgrown gardens pressing in made one feel very much alone. I knew from experience that even the inside of the castle, gorgeously carved and inlaid with gems, was haunted by the same chill and wild flora. Still, I didn't want to take any chances about *extra* hauntings, or extra company on this particular trip. And so I moved on to my next preparation, which William caught wind of with a, "Wait—why do you need *that* one too?"

The Red Horse of the Sun. Contrary to its name, the magic embedded in this little horse had the ability to call down massive storms. All I had to do was hang on to it, think about what I wanted, and suddenly the skies overhead were a roiling gray and with one thunderous *boom* William and I were instantly drenched.

William barked in alarm and leapt for the doorway of the castle. There, huddled against a stone arch, he glared reproachfully up at me. "Would it kill you to give a person *warning?*"

"Sorry," I told him, and I did mean it—but I also couldn't help grinning, if grimly. So far everything was working, and I was more certain with every moment that we were on the right track. "I didn't realize it would be so effective. I'm hoping it'll scare off any meddlers. Keep the bystanders at home, that kind of thing."

"'Meddlers'?" William shook his head in disbelief. "Thought of everything, haven't you."

"I have. Don't forget, in your pack you have the Norse Horse for speed and the *cheval mallet* for its armor properties, because I know you're going to insist on walking in front and looking for traps. I have all the other horses for backup, in addition to lights, snacks, and all the usual 'nerd' accessories."

As usual, William hadn't been listening to my Master Plan. He was stuck upon one of the very first points. "'Norse Horse'?"

"Will you wake up please, and stop repeating everything I

say?" I grinned momentarily to show I was kidding. "I couldn't remember if you decided it was Gullfaxi or Sleipnir, and 'Norse Horse' was easier."

"Look at you, remembering not one but two names!"

"Yeah, well, I—I remember we had a discussion with Luca about it," I mumbled. More like a friendly argument between William and Luca, truthfully, one in which I had no stake. But it had been fun to watch, and I dearly wanted my friend back. Squaring my shoulders, I set back to business. "Okay, first things first: I see the door has overgrown."

It was, indeed, a mass of vines at our back. As we turned to face it, thick leaves waved in the wet wind from the storm.

"Let me guess," said William. "You brought Astarte."

* * *

I had, in fact, brought the limestone carousel horse representing Astarte, goddess of war and fertility. With the little talisman in hand it was as simple as snapping my fingers to make the vines at the castle door wither and shrink away. In no time at all, William and I were inside.

The vaulted ceilings, arched wooden doorways, and dusty, intricate carvings were just as we had left them. The place was filled with silence and the taste of stale air.

"I'm in front," William growled unnecessarily, taking the lead. "Are we doing a sweep or do you have an idea of where he might be?"

"Why would I know?" I glanced through open doorways to my left and right, saw a quickly moving shadow, and gulped. *Probably only the leaves from outside*, I reminded myself. *Outside the vine-covered windows . . .*

The light in the place was a dark, gloomy green. Even my excellent darkvision couldn't be totally trusted. I grabbed a glowstick from my tool belt and shook it, filling the hallway with weak yellow rays.

"You knew him best," William grunted.

"Don't talk in past tense. Maybe we should just yell," I said. "I mean, he's our friend. It's not like there's signs of anyone else being here. Owl's in jail still, after all, and paid thugs would hardly hang around after their boss has been caught. Who else would be around?"

"Fine. On your head be it if something other than Luca answers," William muttered.

I glanced around one more time but my mouth was already open and the shout was in my throat. "Luca! Luca, are you there? It's Red and William! It's safe to come out!"

I waited, holding my breath to hear a response.

The castle around us sighed.

Before William could make a smart comment, a door slammed up ahead and a cold wind blew straight through us. The storm lashed at the door behind us and as I stepped forward, knocking into William, he tumbled and zoomed down the hall.

"Cursed speed," I could hear him sputtering from beyond the reach of my glowstick. As he picked himself up, I decided to try yelling again. Because in theory I'm a smart person, but everyone has their off days . . .

"Luca!" I yelled at the top of my lungs.

This time the wind along the hallway *roared.* William *woofed* back in alarm and I heard a crash from the grand hall he'd disappeared into. I ran ahead, shifting my grip so that in one hand I held a glowstick and in the other I held the porcelain carousel horse Qilin. Because one never knows when one might need a golem.

Qilin could only make teeny tiny golems, but maybe I'd make a swarm of them . . . We'd soon find out.

"William?" I stumbled into the great hall still not having learned my lesson about holding my tongue. In the three-story space, my voice was lost at once. The darkness was thick there, too thick to be natural. I fumbled in my bags for Dispelling Powder when all at once I heard another series of *clangs*.

"Over here—I'm just fine—cursed knight horse!" I heard William gasping, and the scrambling of claws. I ran blindly and nearly fell over what appeared to be an overturned suit of armor. William was on the other side of it, having just freed himself from its weight. He turned to look at me in the dark and no doubt was about to make a witty comment about an armored horse saving him from a suit of armor when, with a *whoosh* and another burst of cold air, he disappeared.

This time I didn't scream. I'd finally learned my lesson. Instead I swung my glowstick wildly, gulping back my shock. There was a hole in the floor under the pedestal the knight had been standing on. That was the only place William could have gone. It seemed to slant down, and make a sort of tunnel. I leaned over to see if I could see William at the bottom. The armor at my feet clanked and whirred and elbowed me firmly in the ribs, then smacked me royally upside my head, and at last I realized that I could either get out of the way or be squished into the wall as the knight resumed his place. Without the charms William carried, I didn't stand a chance.

I leapt free of the armor just in time, breathing hard. At once I began looking for another way to find where William might have gone. The wall the knight had been on was an outer wall; next to it was another overgrown window. I pressed close, my breath fogging the already wavy glass, trying to peer through the vines. There had *definitely* not been this many vines the last time we'd been to the castle. If I put my hands to the glass and squinted, I could just barely see a black smear outside in the rain—

A black smear very much like the shadow which shuddered across my back.

I dropped my hands and my glowstick and whirled at once. There was nothing—nothing that I could see directly. I was alone in a huge room in an even huger castle and my friend had just been locked outside.

But another friend might still be *inside* needing help. I squared my shoulders and moved along the wall. There was nothing for it but to search.

* * *

I made it through exactly one old sitting room, a claustrophobic hallway, and into a music room before I was certain I was being followed.

Maybe not followed exactly, but pursued. Toyed with. As I stood in a doorway shaking, watching, the keys on the ancient piano played themselves, each note tinkling through the haunted space.

Ever since we'd rescued Dusty from the castle basement, he'd insisted the place was cursed—a *real* curse, not just druids being secretive, he'd always said. "No more mysteries for me," he'd say, "I know when a job's too big to take on." I'd heard it a million times.

But I hadn't fully believed him until this moment.

"You don't scare me," I insisted to the clearly-haunted room. Hey, I never said I was honest. "Actually, that's kind of a nice melody."

Outside, the wind howled. Or was it William?

"I need to find my friend," I continued to the possibly-possessed, empty room. Music stands loomed, seeming to bend to my voice. "Two friends, actually. I just want to find them and then I'll be gone."

The piano played dark notes. There was a possibility it was some old spell and not a sentient being that made the music, but I found it unlikely that a remnant like that could be so responsive. *Only one way to find out,* I decided, clutching Qilin. A tiny golem messing with the piano's insides would either end the spell or freak out whoever was there as much as they were freaking out me.

"Fine," I said aloud. "Be that way. But I'm warning you, I'm not leaving this place without them, and my friends will be here any minute!"

Not at the end of the sentence, but somewhere in the middle—right around "leaving"—I brandished Qilin like some kind of magic wand. A molten little rock-man went flying from my hand and *splatted* against the piano, creating a moment of absolute silence in which I realized I had no idea how to make the golem actually *do* anything, particularly investigate a haunted instrument. My frantic musings were interrupted by the smell of smoke.

"Oh, goddess preserve me," I whispered, an old favorite curse of my mother's. How could I have overlooked the fact that molten rock and wooden instrument might not mix? "I didn't mean to do that, sorry, you see I'm just very focused on finding my friends and if you would *help* instead of being creepy, then—"

A gust of frigid air stole away my breath and cut me off mid-word. The piano, no, the *castle* roared and shook. Knickknacks began shivering off shelves. The darkness plummeted toward absolute black. A disembodied, horribly raspy voice said,

"GET OUT!"

Taking all of this as a sign that my apology was not accepted, I turned on my heel and ran.

I sprinted back through the hallway and crossed the sitting room in two bounds, emerging into the foyer still breathless. I paused for only a moment. One way I'd been, one way I'd just come from. I didn't want to go upstairs—that would be even farther from William's potential help. That left one option. I tucked my head and darted for the back of the castle, where I knew from experience that an old greenhouse could be found smushed right up against the old wood and stone.

As my feet skidded across the wooden floors, the shaking of the walls and the freezing wind continued. I realized mid-hallway that a glass greenhouse might not be a good place to be if more things started breaking, but it was too late now. I was committed. I was even more committed when I realized that at the end of the hallway, there were double doors leading into the greenhouse. I had no idea who was after me or if they were even corporeal, but still, I had to try. I gathered up every scrap of speed and agility my mothers had taught me and I flung myself through the doorway only to spin and slam the doors behind me.

The wind made a noise like thunder against the heavy wooden doors. But most of it was left in the hall. Quickly, breathlessly, my fingers slipping amongst my many pockets, I slipped an Evertrue Chain from its hiding place on my belt and tied the doorhandles closed.

I breathed a huge gulp of relief as I stepped back. The ghostly wind was only a sigh at the floorboards beneath the doors. The rattling was firmly on the other side of the wall. Whatever was chasing me, it had fallen prey to my plan.

Or so I thought. Then I turned around and saw bright green eyes.

I must have simultaneously screamed and gone momentarily deaf—the two may or may not have been related—because without warning, William crashed through the glass behind the apparition. I don't remember hearing the impact, but I remember being dazzled by the spray of raindrops, glass, and dirt in William's blue protective glow. Overgrown houseplants and pots went flying. Words, too, started bouncing all over the room:

"Red!"

"William!!"

"Rrremain calm—"

"Wait, are you Jade? Jade, have you been haunting me this entire time?" That didn't make any sense. Jade, a local ghost, had always been helpful. Even if William had always been suspicious about the apparition. My mind continued to race, my heartbeat still petrified.

"Get away from Red!"

"Give me the wind horrrse, or you will not find yourr friend—"

"Out of my way!!"

"Why would you want to stop us finding Luca?" *The ghost horse, why would you want the ghost horse? Why would you want to scare us and hurt our friend?* I couldn't voice all my questions at once.

"—I *must* have the horrrse—"

"—why would *you* want a horse?" *Is someone making you do this? Did you want this all along? Were you working with Owl? Why did you help me? Were you always going to steal—*

"This ends now!"

With William's authoritative bark, the room was filled with starry light. As though caught in a flash of lightning, there we were: me, still stunned, poised by the door; those eyes and pointed ears which I knew as 'Jade' floating in the middle of the forested room; and William about to lunge. Then like a roll of thunder we all tumbled down together. Freezing hands tore at my arms and my tunic, dragging me forward. William's paws flailed through empty air. More plants crashed, and the vials in my utility belt crashed, and wooden planks in the floor below us crashed, sending us lurching down into the dark folly of what once had been a shallow well. We were wet—soaked—almost drowning; but the water feature had long dried up. I sputtered like a cat thrown into the bath, my hands reaching out to capture not Jade, not William, but the little carousel horse that had fallen from my pocket. Uchaishravas, the King of Horses and carrier of Elixir of Life.

"Would you stop doing that with that thing?" William growled. His tail smacked me upside the head as he stood and tuned in the little space we'd fallen into. A space all the smaller because someone else was there with us. "Where'd your ghost 'friend' go? I told you that thing was bad news!"

"Red? William?" Luca's voice was breathless.

"Th—the horses," I stammered, unable to process anything else. In the milky light from the magicked water and William's aura, they were illuminated. I was on my hands and knees in six inches of water, magic water which had probably saved me from injury falling down into this well, impervious to any danger or hurts. I was watching the horses. In the undulating, uncertain light, it looked like they were moving.

"William," I whispered hoarsely, "you — you dropped yours." I had dropped mine, too, of course. In the fight and ensuing fall, I'd dropped just about everything. My utility belt lay like a dead snake beside me, and my satchel was in shreds. All those pockets and precautions, gone. But for some reason it suddenly struck me as funny that *William* had dropped his cargo, too. Where had he been carrying them in the first place? How could magical pockets fail?

I would have laughed, but the sound caught in my throat. It died, because there was another sound to listen to—something beyond the lapping of water or the shuffling of William's furry feet. There was singing. There was music.

And the horses were still moving.

They'd come together, all nine of them laid out in a circle. *There's no way,* I thought, no longer able to voice my thoughts. *No way they just landed like that. They're being drawn—drawn together somehow . . .*

And that's when I noticed the light was growing.

No longer coming from William or the mess around us, light shone down through the storm, through the greenhouse, into the well. Like a holy benediction it landed precisely in the middle of the ring of carousel horses. And as I watched it, unbelieving, I blinked and saw that there was another horse there, a tenth one. A horse I had never seen before, prancing in the middle of its circle of companions.

It was so, so simple, that little horse. Almost comically

so. It had none of the mysterious lacquer or carved rosettes or golden accents that the other horses had. It was just a luminescent white, the kind of white that isn't even a color at all—and yet, is tinged with every other color in existence. The other horses were sandstone or azurite or abalone. This horse was holy water and purified flame.

And it spoke with a voice that I did not hear, but instead felt deep in my heart:

Nine together, and I will come,
  As round and round the stories ring true.
  Take never all, but take some,
  The music remembers a world split in two.

Truth and tales, together and apart,
  The world is never one,
  Round and round, near and far,
  Always beginning, rarely done.

Seek and find, but I always know,
  And I sing the truth into being,
  Up and down, to and fro,
  Stand alone, others are fleeing.

"It's a riddle," said Luca very softly at my shoulder. "Owl thought the horses would reveal a truth about the world that he could use. Something to make him 'stand alone,' I suppose."

I didn't move. *Ruin the world,* that's what I'd been told the horses could do. Maybe what they really did was ruin illusions. "Use against who?"

"Against everyone." Luca rustled regretfully, then chuckled.

"Who else?"

Across from us, William shook himself. "Right, well, there's the mystery of *Why Red the Seer-Who-Doesn't-Believe-in-Fate Attracted a Bunch of Charmed Horses* solved. I think I hear the others shouting. Put those things away and figure out how we're getting out of here, because I'm not sharing any more insights with you until I'm warm and dry."

* * *

One awkward climb, very long walk, steaming shower, and heaping platter of toasted sandwiches later, I informed William, "I still don't really believe in fate."

"Great. So we're still going to get weird lore knocking down our door, because that's exactly how a 'world split in two' works. Dualities attract each other," he returned. He was taking up the vast majority of the living room rug, while Luca and I shared my tiny sofa. Ryuko and Cairn had gone back to their homes, and Thorn was busy with paperwork at the station.

The rain I hadn't been able to stop lashed at my windows, and tea steamed on the sidetable. I breathed deep, reminding myself that it didn't matter if William was going to be a grump: I could still enjoy this moment.

"The only fate I believe in," I continued lightly, "is what I'll be wreaking if I ever see Jade again. I can't *believe* that coward's nerve, acting like a friend and then betraying us like that. Probably Jade was with Owl all along. Is that what was keeping you in that well, Luca?"

"Well, I did go to the castle on my own—to hide, you know,

when I saw how things were going with Owl at the shop." Luca was half-hiding behind his sandwich, his voice smaller than normal. "But then there was . . . you called the ghost 'Jade'?"

"I have no idea what or who Jade is," I admitted. "I just gave it that nickname because of the green eyes."

"A ghost would make sense," said William, "since Red spilling the Elixir of Life everywhere seemed to scare it off. Interacting with a charm like that would be enough to banish a ghost, at least for a little while, I'd say."

"Long enough to not get in our way, which is for the best," I said. My indignation and betrayal softened a little when I looked to Luca, who was still taking everything in.

"Yeah," he agreed limply, nodding slowly, ". . . you're right, Red."

"You have to be at least *some* of the time," William grumped.

"Jade talked to me once about justice," I said, distracted. "I still can't get over it. What kind of justice is it, letting Owl get hold of some crazy magic?"

"Not justice, truth," William corrected. "Maybe the truth of the matter is that your pal Jade wanted the opposite of what you did."

"To flee," Luca said very softly. "That's what was in the song, right? 'Others fleeing' . . . maybe it's a kind of banishment too."

"But when we put the horses together, even accidentally, they didn't actually do anything," I said, looking to William for confirmation. "That happened after Jade disappeared."

William sneezed. "They *did* do something, Red. They revealed a truth to you."

"The truth of what?" I blinked.

"'A world split in two,'" Luca mused.

William just stared at us smugly.

"Okay, fine, I'll bite," I said at last, chuckling. Though Dusty's old advice about curses rang in my ears, I never seem to know when a job is too big. "What's your expert opinion on all this, William?"

"You have to start at the beginning to get it. Someone made the little statues—a sorcerer most likely, and a crazy one at that. That doesn't matter so much since it would have been centuries ago now. When charms are around that long, they start to take on a life of their own. The horses grew in power because the myths they represented were repeated year after year, like a carousel repeating. See? "

"Not unlike yourself?" Luca asked with a sly grin. I winked at him, glad to see his spirits rising.

William ignored both of us. "That original creation spell created a bond that kept them linked even when they were apart. But the important thing to note is that the truth they were created to uphold—the world-destroying truth which was supposed to be revealed when they all came together, which we now know was Owl's goal all along—regarded the *duality* of existence. That was the whole point: that two things can be true at once, and furthermore, that you're more powerful when you work with that fact rather than trying to 'stand alone.' 'Others fleeing' is a *bad* thing—it means you're falling behind the real world."

"I get it," Luca said eagerly. "Like how the statuettes were both harmless toys and dangerous talismans, or how each one both represented a myth and was its own creation. How a carousel moves but stays in place. Two things at once."

"And that's also why they as magical entities were attracted to one who rejected magic. Ergo, Red," William added, pausing dramatically. Then he added, thoughtfully, "And me, of course. Perhaps it was the combination of both of us, since *I* was the one who could identify them all."

This time both Luca and I laughed. "I don't think I'll ever fully understand," I admitted, and said to Luca, "Maybe you can be Thorn's new assistant instead of me, since you're so smart."

From under his terry robe hood, he grinned back at me. "You better watch out, Red. You'll be regretting those words when I become Belville's new mystery-solver extraordinaire instead of you."

"I'm just fine with my life of peace and boring quiet, thanks."

"Which I just said is an illusion," William insisted, "if you would ever listen to me or show an interest in the arcane. These kinds of things are *attracted* to you, Red."

And I thought then, in my cozy apartment surrounded by friends, that if on occasion weird or even dangerous things might be attracted to me, that it might be okay. Jade had said to me once that carousels were meant to uphold fantasies. And I knew now that what I'd have to do, to stay sane in this crazy merry-go-round of life in Belville, was keep sight of the things in my life that were real.

In the next few days, summer began to ease into fall, sorcerers and pixies flew off to their homes, and life eased back into routine. After Luca's recovery and evidence, Owl finally confessed to his scheme. In time, he'd be put on trial. Meanwhile, Luca himself picked up the pieces and went out reopening the bookstore, this time not as clerk but as scholar in his own right.

We never did talk very much about his time at the castle, or how he'd ended up in that well. He must have told Thorn, of course, but I didn't like to ask him about it. And we didn't hear so much as a whispery 'boo' from Jade, either. Accomplice, victim, or mastermind—there was no way to tell exactly what Jade had been.

Of course, this didn't sit well with William, who insisted on keeping up all his wards on the carousel horses. But somehow, I found it didn't bother me. Perhaps part of me didn't want to know for sure. Or perhaps, with the mystery of the carousel horses' purpose solved, I didn't mind if another went unsolved for now.

As some might say—it was much too big for me to take on.

After all, as William himself pointed out, the very nature of our world isn't just one thing or another. It's both at the same time.

Reference: Mythological Horses

I've done my best to organize my notes and research on all the horses involved in the Capers (though I'm sure to have missed some details here or there!). In methodical order, here are all the little gems of knowledge necessary for you, like William, to amaze and astound your friends!

The First Horse

Name: *Caballo marino chilote*

Type: siren-like water horse, similar to kelpie, backahast, nixie, wihwin, and others

Cultural Origin: Chilean

Story of Origin? Local ghost/creature lore

Strengths: swimming, carrying sorcerers to ghost ships, looking very pretty

Weaknesses: generally subservient to sorcerers

Description & Folklore: The caballo marino chilote originates in the folklore of Chile, where it is said that these sea-horses ferry sorcerers across the waves. Often they are invisible, but if you are lucky enough to see one, it might have a golden mane and a long, fish-like tail (sometimes in addition to its rear feet). Some version of this creature appears in many world cultures, including Greek (hippocampus) and Scottish (kelpie). Though they can be beautiful, they're very dangerous.

The Second Horse

Name: the Red Horse of the Sun
   Type: godly mount
   Cultural Origin: Diné (or Navajo)
   Story of Origin? the Glacier Song of Horses
   Strengths: traversing the sky, riding through storms
   Weaknesses: bound to the Sun-God
Description & Folklore: "The Glacier Song of Horses" describes the five horses of the Sun-God: a horse of turquoise, a horse of white shell, one of pearly shell, one of red shell, and one of coal. While the Sun-God may ride one of the first three during good weather, if there are storms, he rides the red horse or the horse of coal. Other related stories include similar symbolism between the colors of the horses and the directions North, South, East, and West. In my research I found several versions of this story, and of course I added twists of my own as well. I suggest looking into navajopeople.org or The Legend of the Horse by Don Mose Jr as authorities on the subject!

The Third Horse

Name: Horse of Power
   Type: invincible talking horse
   Cultural Origin: Russian
   Story of Origin? The Firebird, The Horse of Power, and the
Princess Vasilissa
   Strengths: knowing how to accomplish impossible tasks, running without tiring, having hooves of iron
   Weaknesses: none to speak of (unless "having a rider who

doesn't always listen" counts)

Description & Folklore: The Horse of Power is one of the main characters in the Russian fairy tale "The Firebird, the Horse of Power, and the Princess Vasilissa," and others like it. In these stories, the Horse of Power assists a young man who is given three impossible tasks. Each time, the young man is sure that he will die, but his horse knows what to do and gives him precise instructions. It is said that the Horse of Power is descended from the great horses of long ago, who have disappeared now; and that he has eyes like fire, hooves of iron, and a thundering, unmatchable pace.

The Norse Horse

Name: Gullfaxi or Sleipnir
  Type: godly mount (perhaps even a demigod)
  Cultural Origin: Norse
  Story of Origin? various
  Strengths: incredible speed, reliability in battle
  Weaknesses: subservient to Thor and Odin respectively
Description & Folklore: Sleipnir, or "the sliding one," came first. Born of a giant's horse and the god Loki, Sleipnir belonged to Odin, and was said to be the fastest horse in all the realms. Many myths say Sleipnir actually had eight legs. Meanwhile, Gullfaxi ("golden mane") belonged to another of the giants, who dared to race him against Odin and Sleipnir. The race ended in a battle and the giant was killed, so Gullfaxi went to Thor's son. Both horses are described as beautiful, faster than the wind, and more valuable than many of the treasures of the world.

The Fifth Horse

Name: Wind Horse
 Type: spiritual guide
 Cultural Origin: East and Central Asian
 Story of Origin? various
 Strengths: signifying goodness or luck, guiding souls
 Weaknesses: usually incorporeal
Description & Folklore: Today, the Wind Horse is most often associated with early Tibetan or Buddhist mythologies. It's a symbol of the essence of good luck, "basic goodness," and the movement of or changes in the soul. It's a powerful symbol of good, but it is intangible and can't be tamed. The strong and brave may harness and ride it, however, and we would say they're "making their own luck" or enjoying good fortune. The Wind Horse does appear on a prayer flag, as Gilbert references in the story, along with other animals representing the elements and well-being. In Mongolia, the wind horse's name has become synonymous with soul. It's often depicted with wings.

The Sixth Horse

Name: *le cheval mallet*
 Type: siren-like horse (*sans* water)
 Cultural Origin: French
 Story of Origin? Local ghost/creature lore
 Strengths: looking very regal, running straight to hell
 Weaknesses: complete lack of compassion for folks who want to disembark

Description & Folklore: The cheval mallet is, as William observes, very similar to the more-familiar kelpie. It is rumored to be extremely beautiful and attired in only the finest saddle and bridle. Usually, it is white or black. The cheval will appear only during the middle of the night, when it approaches weary travelers who are walking home alone. If the traveler sees the horse and thinks 'finally! A ride home!' and gets on, they'll never be seen or heard from again. The legend goes that once you're on the cheval mallet, you can't get off, no matter how hard you try; and the horse will proceed to take you straight to the underworld. So beware of fancy horses alone on the road at night!

The Seventh Horse

Name: Qilin, Ch'i-lin, Ky-lin, K'i-lin
   Type: unicorn-like elemental creature
   Cultural Origin: Chinese
   Story of Origin? various
   Strengths: prophesying a virtuous leader, symbolizing perfection among land animals
   Weaknesses: extremely rare
   Description & Folklore: Though Qilin is often called "the Chinese unicorn," truthfully this creature is very different from the unicorns we're familiar with in the West. Traditional reports of Qilin say it has the head of a lion, the tail of a dragon, the body of a goat, and it may even be covered in scales or feathers. It's also usually very colorful. Like other unicorns, Qilin is very powerful, gentle, and just. It's sometimes said to dwell at the center of the earth. My version of Qilin

masquerades as a porcelain carousel horse, as porcelain is a Chinese invention created at extremely high temperatures.

The Eighth Horse

Name: the horse of Astarte
  Type: godly mount or symbol
  Cultural Origin: Ancient Near East/Ancient Egypt
  Story of Origin? various
  Strengths: heralding righteousness or success in war, healing
  Weaknesses: subservient to Astarte
Description & Folklore: The goddess Astarte (also Ashtart or Athtart) was a powerful member of the Ancient Near Eastern pantheon, generally said to represent war, royalty, sex, and sometimes fertility or hunting. She was associated with both the lion and the horse (and chariot). As the horse was one of her symbols, rather than a specific named creature, in my story I treated the limestone horse essentially as a messenger of Astarte.

The Ninth Horse

Name: Uchaishravas, King of Horses
  Type: godly mount
  Cultural Origin: Hindu
  Story of Origin? various
  Strengths: being the best of all horses, association with the Ocean of Milk (and therefore the Nectar of Immortal Life)
  Weaknesses: might also be the horse of a demon

Description & Folklore: Uchaishravas is an impressive sight, said to have seven heads, a pure white coat, and the ability to fly. He was born from the Ocean of Milk, a mystical place which also created Lakshmi (goddess of fortune) and the Nectar of Immortal Life, among other treasures. In some stories, he is the horse of the gods–but there are some tales, too, where he is ridden by a demon. Whoever his rider, Uchaishravas is the prototype and apex of what all horses can be.

The Final Horse

Name: Horse of Light
  Type: unicorn
  Cultural Origin: Ancient Greece, Western Europe
  Story of Origin? various
  Strengths: signaling virtue, healing, protecting wild forests
  Weaknesses: extremely rare
  Description & Folklore: Our last mythical horse is perhaps the simplest: the unicorn. Red and her friends think of it as the Horse of Light, because its actual shape and color are vague and ethereal–something I thought fitting, since through the centuries there have been *many* conceptions of what a unicorn might look like. Today, unicorns are familiar as symbols of individuality and beauty, often accompanied by rainbows. But historically, unicorns were associated with elusive wildness, a creature both familiar and very strange. To some, they also symbolized purity, virginity, and various saints, gods, or royals. For my part, I like that the unicorn can be both fierce and gentle, a fighter or a healer, and extremely rare yet likely to pop up on a sticker, shirt or cupcake at any time.

Coloring Book Access and Advice

Want even *more* mythological horses? (Me too!) Enjoy exclusive access to a special ebook of coloring pages inspired by each of the horses in these stories. Feel free to download, print, and beautify the illustrations to your heart's content!

Find the coloring book by entering this into your search bar:

https://ellehartford.com/stories/carousel-coloring-book/

And use this as your password:

Carousel2022

The best advice I can give you for coloring is just to sharpen your pencils, dive in, and have fun!

Advice
from a carousel horse

Know your own power.

Keep moving forward.

Appreciate fine details and fancy accessories now and then!

Take life's ups and downs in stride.

Don't be afraid to be colorful.

Keep magic in your heart.

Enjoy the ride!

Looking Back: The Start of a Wild Ride

Where did this all begin?

Well . . .

To me, as an author, Red's world is an intersection of two things I love: fantasy and history. It may seem a strange connection, but a lot of Red's alchemy is based on old (think Ancient Greek) proto-science, and of course your average fairy tale village is basically medieval in its day-to-day life. When I first started writing stories about Red and her friends, I was actually employed as a "Historian and Miller" at a small historical site.

(And yes, we did actually grind grain with millstones. It was *very* historic!)

Through work, I happened to meet a lot of other history-minded folk. Birds of a feather, and all! One such bird was a funny academic with a penchant for button-down shirts rivaled only by his love of joining historic committees. If you've read any Jeeves & Wooster, then you already have the perfect picture in your mind.

(I had read *lots* of Jeeves & Wooster by that point, and I knew a good egg when I saw one.)

So, given that my boyfriend and I had been brought together by a love of history, what did we do when on holiday? Why, went to historic sites, of course. And antique stores. *Many* antique stores. The kind that stretch on for miles and miles, it seems, and in each case or corner or well-worn stall is a collection of items from a different seller.

We were at one such store in Pennsylvania and I'd just started writing mystery stories. To be honest, I was probably just counting my steps until we got home so I could work on my latest idea—maybe even one of Red's early stories, like "The Witch's Brew" or "The Alchemical Godmother." I'd made it all the way through the store—more like a warehouse—glancing at dusty plates and pawing through faded books. I was about to leave empty-handed when I came upon a little round cabinet along the far wall.

I remember the cabinet perfectly because it was the perfect container for carousel horses. Glass all the way around, with little mirrored shelves. Plenty of light and space for mystery.

The horses themselves weren't arranged with any particular care other than *it's past time these were sold.* There were ten of them, all jumbled up and facing different directions, scattered across the various levels. Though it was clear they were of a collection, the only things they had in common were their gold poles and their size, just a little bigger than the palm of my hand.

Now, I'm an author, and a fantasy author at that, so it may not surprise you to learn that I like symbols. I spent *ages* trying to pick which two horses appealed to me most, based on what stories they might symbolize. Just two, mind you, because I also like budgets. My boyfriend, who likes adhering to schedules and not staying in stores past closing time, became a little impatient waiting.

(Don't worry, he's used to it by now.)

Well, I picked my favorite two eventually—the lovely white horse which later inspired Sleipnir in "A Gold Shadow," and the enigmatic black steed which could only be the Talking Horse in "An Iron Voice." (It really does have a phoenix painted on its side!) The nice people at the antiques store boxed them up for me, of course, but I promptly unboxed them. That evening at our hotel, the horses were on the coffee table during games; and all night they were on my dresser. I was enchanted.

Normally, enchanted or not, I try to make a decision and stick to it. But this time that wasn't working for me. On the last day of our trip, I told my boyfriend I wanted to go back to the antiques store. Surely, I'd decided, any budget must have room for an extra blue glass horse (later the *caballo marino*) and perhaps a pearly red one (sure to be the Red Horse of the Sun God) too.

(Now, what I didn't know at the time was that he *also* wanted to go back to that store, and that I had rather ruined his plans by revisiting my decision.)

There were four of us on this journey to the antiques store: me, my boyfriend, and his parents. Normally his parents are wonderful people. On this particular shopping trip, they were—how should I say it . . . overly solicitous? Chatty? A bit annoying? I didn't think too much of it at the time, to be honest, but of course now we see how important that bit of information was—just like one of Agatha Christie's clues!

Needless to say, by the time I made it to the glass cabinet, the horses were gone.

I was disappointed, naturally, but I chalked it up as a lesson—*act now or regret it later!*—and soldiered on. We went home, and I wrote more stories, and Belville began to take shape.

And then, on Valentine's Day, a white carousel horse decorated with rosettes showed up.

And on my birthday, a black knight's horse with gold edging on his fine saddle cloth.

And for perhaps no occasion at all, a finely made porcelain horse pranced along.

Of course, by *that* point I understood what was up. (I do spend a lot of time thinking about mysteries, after all.) And I think, by then, I'd begun writing the carousel stories already. I remember very vividly researching lists of mythological horses (because I am a nerd, but not *so* big a nerd I knew all about these horses to begin with!) and matching myths to carousel statues, like a whimsical elementary school game. It was the most fun I've ever had writing short stories, to be honest, and I think part of the reason was that *I wasn't doing it alone.*

All ten carousel horses now roam our little house freely, perched on windowsills and cavorting on mantles. And all ten stories are done—no more last minute edits or additions, which, let me tell you, is a very difficult fact to face!

These days my life is filled with more fantasy than history, and the boyfriend who seemed to be a perpetual student is starting his teaching career. If I see something I want at an antiques store, I know to buy it now rather than regret it later (though my boyfriend still prides himself on having surprised me for my birthday, this time with a party rather than a horse). A lot of change happened during these stories, behind the scenes. But they still bring me so much joy, in part because—as William hinted—they represent an overlap of things I love. History and fantasy. Fictional friends and real ones.

In short, real life—and magic.

About the Author

Elle adores cozy mysteries, horses of all stripes, and above all, learning new things. As a historian and educator, she believes in the value of stories as a mirror for complicated realities. She currently lives in New Jersey with a grumpy tortoise and a three-legged cat.

Find more stories of Red and her friends at ellehartford.com. And while you're there, sign up for Elle's newsletter to get bonus material, behind-the-scenes sneak peeks, and terrible jokes!

You can connect with me on:
- https://ellehartford.com
- https://twitter.com/HartfordElle
- https://www.facebook.com/ElleHartfordAuthor

Subscribe to my newsletter:
- https://beyondwriting.eo.page/newsletter